Books by Albert Camus

Awarded the Nobel Prize for Literature in 1957

These are Borzoi books,
published in New York by Alfred A. Knopf

A
Happy
Death

"Cahier I"

A Happy Death

by Albert Camus

Translated from the French by Richard Howard

Afterword and Notes by Jean Sarocchi

Alfred A. Knopf New York 1972

Library of Congress Cataloging in Publication Data
Camus, Albert, 1913–1960. A happy death.
(His Cahier 1) Translation of La mort heureuse. I. Title.
PZ3.C1574Hap3 [PQ2605.A3734] 843'.9'14 78–171141
ISBN 0-394-47262-4

Contents

Part One

Natural Death

1

It was ten in the morning, and Patrice Mersault was walking steadily toward Zagreus' villa. By now the housekeeper had left for the market, and the villa was deserted. It was a beautiful April morning, chilly and bright; the sky was radiant, but there was no warmth in the glistening sunshine. The empty road sloped up toward the villa, and a pure light streamed between the pines covering the hillside. Patrice Mersault was carrying a suitcase, and as he walked on through that primal morning, the only sounds he heard were the click of his own footsteps on the cold road and the regular creak of the suitcase handle.

Not far from the villa, the road crossed a little square decorated with flowerbeds and benches. The effect of the early red geraniums among gray aloes, the blue sky, and the whitewashed walls was so fresh, so childlike that Mersault stopped a moment before walking on through the square. Then the road sloped down again toward Zagreus' villa. On the doorstep he paused and put on his gloves. He opened the door which the cripple never locked and carefully closed it behind him. He walked down the hall to the third door on the left, knocked and went in. Zagreus was there, of course, a blanket over the stumps of his legs, sitting in an armchair by the fire exactly where Mersault had sat two days ago. He was reading, and his book lay open on the blanket; there was no surprise in his round eyes as he stared up at Mersault, who was standing in front of the closed door. The curtains were drawn back, and patches of sunshine lay on the floor, the furniture, making objects glitter in the room. Beyond the window, the morning rejoiced over the cold, golden earth. A great icy joy, the birds' shrill, tentative outcry, the flood of pitiless light gave the day an aspect of innocence and truth. Mersault stood motionless, the room's stifling heat filling his throat, his ears. Despite the change in the weather, there was a blazing fire in the grate. And Mersault felt his blood rising to his temples, pounding at the tips of his ears. Zagreus' eyes followed his movements, though he did not say a word. Patrice walked toward the chest on the other side of the fireplace and put his suitcase down on a table without looking at the cripple. He felt a faint tremor in his ankles now. He took out a cigarette and lit it—clumsily, for he was wearing gloves. A faint noise behind him made him turn around, the cigarette between his lips. Zagreus was still staring at him, but had just closed the book. Mersault—the fire was painfully hot against his knees now—could read the title upside down: *The Courtier* by Baltasar Gracián. Then he bent over the chest and opened it. The revolver was still there, its lustrous black, almost feline curves on the white letter. Mersault picked up the envelope with his left hand and the revolver with his right. After an instant's hesitation, he thrust the gun under his left arm and opened the envelope. It contained one large sheet of paper, with only a few lines of Zagreus' tall, angular handwriting across the top:

"I am doing away with only half a man. It need cause no problem—there is more than enough here to pay off those who have taken care of me till now. Please use what is left over to improve conditions of the men in death row. But I know it's asking a lot."

Expressionless, Mersault folded the sheet and put it back in the envelope. As he did so the smoke from his cigarette stung his eyes, and a tiny chunk of ash fell on the envelope. He shook it off, set the envelope on the table where it was sure to be noticed, and turned toward Zagreus, who was staring at the envelope now, his stubby powerful fingers still holding the book. Mersault bent down, turned the key of the little strongbox inside the chest, and took out the packets of bills, only their ends visible in the newspaper wrappings. Holding the gun under one arm, with the other hand he methodically filled up the suitcase. There were fewer than twenty packets of hundreds, and Mersault realized he had brought too large a suitcase. He left one packet in the safe. Then he closed the suitcase, flicked the half-smoked cigarette into the fire and, taking the revolver in his right hand, walked toward the cripple.

Zagreus was staring at the window now. A car drove slowly past, making a faint chewing sound.

Motionless, Zagreus seemed to be contemplating all the inhuman beauty of this April morning. When he felt the barrel against his right temple, he did not turn away. But Patrice, watching him, saw his eyes fill with tears. It was Patrice who closed his eyes. He stepped back and fired. Leaning against the wall for a moment, his eyes still closed, he felt his blood throbbing in his ears. Then he opened his eyes. The head had fallen over onto the left shoulder, the body only slightly tilted. But it was no longer Zagreus he saw now, only a huge, bulging wound of brain, blood, and bone. Mersault began to tremble. He walked around to the other side of the armchair, groped for Zagreus' right hand, thrust the revolver into it, raised it to the temple, and let it fall back. The revolver dropped onto the arm of the chair and then into Zagreus' lap. Now Mersault noticed the cripple's mouth and chin—he had the same serious and sad expression as when he was staring at the window. Just then a shrill horn sounded in front of the door. A second time. Mersault, still leaning over the armchair, did not move. The sound of tires meant that the butcher had driven away. Mersault picked up his suitcase, turned the doorknob gleaming suddenly in a sunbeam, and left the room, his head throbbing, his mouth parched. He opened the outer door and walked away quickly. There was no one in sight except a group of children at one end of the little square. He walked on. Past the square, he was suddenly aware of the cold, and shivered under his light jacket. He sneezed twice, and the valley filled with shrill mocking echoes that the crystal sky carried higher and higher. Staggering slightly, he stopped and took a deep breath. Millions of tiny white smiles thronged down from the blue sky. They played over the leaves still cupping the rain, over the damp earth of the paths, soared to the blood-red tile roofs, then back into the lakes of air and light from which they had just overflowed. A tiny plane hummed its way across the sky. In this flowering of air, this fertility of the heavens, it seemed as if a man's one duty was to live and be happy. Everything in Mersault fell silent. He sneezed a third time, and shivered feverishly. Then he hurried away without glancing around him, the suitcase creaking, his footsteps loud on the road. Once he was back in his room and had put the suitcase in a corner, he lay down on his bed and slept until the middle of the afternoon.

2

Summer crammed the harbor with noise and sunlight. It was eleven thirty. The day split open down
the middle, crushing the docks under the burden of
its heat. Moored at the sheds of the Algiers Munici-
pal Depot, black-hulled, red-chimneyed freighters
were loading sacks of wheat. Their dusty fragrance
mingled with the powerful smell of tar melting under a hot sun. Men were drinking at a little stall that
reeked of creosote and anisette, while some Arab
acrobats in red shirts somersaulted on the scorching
flagstones in front of the sea in the leaping light.
Without so much as a glance at them, the stevedores
carrying the sacks walked up the two sagging planks
that slanted from the dock to the freighter decks.
When they reached the top, their silhouettes were
suddenly divided between the sea and the sky
among the winches and masts. They stopped for an
instant, dazzled by the light, eyes gleaming in the
whitish crust of dust and sweat that covered their
faces, before they plunged blindly into the hold
stinking of hot blood. In the fiery air, a siren blew
without stopping.

Suddenly the men on the plank stopped in con-
fusion. One of them had fallen, and was caught between the planks, his arm pinned under his body,
crushed under the tremendous weight of the sack,
and he screamed with pain. Just at this moment,

Patrice Mersault emerged from his office, and on the doorstep, the summer heat took his breath away. He opened his mouth, inhaled the tar vapors, which stung his throat, and then he went over to the stevedores. They had moved the man who had been hurt, and he was lying in the dust, his lips white with pain, his arm dangling, broken above the elbow. A sliver of bone had pierced the flesh, making an ugly wound from which blood was dripping. The drops rolled down his arm and fell, one by one, onto the scorching stones with a tiny hiss, and turned to steam. Mersault was staring, motionless, at the blood when someone took his arm. It was Emmanuel, one of the clerks. He pointed to a truck heading toward them with a salvo of backfires. "That one?" Patrice began to run as the truck drove past them, chains rattling. They dashed after it, swallowed up by dust and noise, panting and blind, just conscious enough to feel themselves swept on by the frenzied effort of running, in a wild rhythm of winches and machines, accompanied by the dancing masts on the horizon and the pitching of the leprous hulls they passed. Mersault was the first to grab hold, confident of his strength and skill, and he jumped onto the moving truck. He helped Emmanuel up, and the two men sat with their legs dangling in the chalk-white dust, while a luminous suffocation poured out of the sky over the circle of the harbor crowded with masts and black cranes, the uneven cobbles of the dock jarring Emmanuel and Mersault as the truck gained speed, making them laugh until they were breathless, dizzied by the jolting movement, the searing sky, their own boiling blood.

When they reached Belcourt, Mersault slid off with Emmanuel, who was singing now, loud and out of tune. "You know," he told Mersault, "it comes up in your chest. It comes when you feel good. When you're in the water." It was true: Emmanuel sang when he swam, and his voice, hoarse from shouting, inaudible against the sea, marked time for the gestures of his short, muscular arms. They were walking down the rue de Lyon, Mersault tall beside Emmanuel, his broad shoulders rolling. In the way he stepped onto the curb, the way he twisted his hips to avoid the crowd that occasionally closed in on him, his body seemed curiously young and vigorous, capable of bearing him to any extreme of physical joy. Relaxed, he rested his weight on one hip with a self-conscious litheness, like a man whose body has acquired its style from sports. His eyes sparkled under the heavy brows, and as he talked to Emmanuel he would tug at his collar with a mechanical gesture to free his neck muscles, tensing his curved mobile lips at the same time. They walked into their restaurant, sat down at a table, and ate in silence. It was cool inside, among the flies, the clatter of plates, the hum of conversation. The owner, Celeste, a tall man with huge mustaches, walked over to greet them, scratching his belly under his apron. "Pretty good," Celeste answered them, "good for an old man." Celeste and Emmanuel exchanged exclamations and thumped each other on the shoulder. "Old men," Celeste said, "you know what old men are, they're all the same. Shitheads. They tell you a real man's got to be fifty. But that's because *they're* fifty. I knew this one guy who could have his good times just with his son. They'd go out together. On the town. They'd go to the Casino, and this guy would say: 'Why should I hang around with a lot of old men! Every day they tell me they've taken some medicine, there's always something wrong with their liver. I have a better time with my son. Sometimes he picks up a whore, I look the other way, I take the streetcar. So long and thanks. Fine with me.' " Emmanuel laughed. "Of course," Celeste said, "the guy was no authority, but I liked him all right." He turned to Mersault. "Anyway, it's better than this other guy I knew. When he made his money, he would talk with his head way up making gestures all the time. Now he's not so proud of himself—he's lost it all."

"Serves him right," Mersault said.

"Oh, you can't be a bastard in life. This guy took it while he had it, and he was right. Almost a million francs he had . . . Now if it had been me!"

"What would you do?" Emmanuel asked.

"I'd buy myself a cabin on the beach, I'd put some glue in my navel, and I'd stick a flag in there. Then I'd wait to see which way the wind was blowing."

Mersault ate quietly until Emmanuel started to tell Celeste how he had fought the battle of the Marne. "See, they sent us Zouaves out in front . . ."

"Cut the bullshit," Mersault said calmly.

"The major said, 'Charge!' and we ran down into a kind of gully, only with trees in it. He told us to charge, but no one was there. So we just marched right on, kept on walking. And then all of a sudden these machineguns are firing right into us. We all fall on top of each other. There were so many dead and wounded that you could have rowed a boat across the blood in that gully. Some of them kept screaming, 'Mama!' Christ, it was awful."

Mersault stood up and tied a knot in his napkin. The owner walked over to the kitchen door and chalked the price of his dinner on it. When one of his customers hadn't paid up, Celeste would take the door off its hinges and bring the evidence on his back. René, his son, was eating a boiled egg over in a corner. "Poor kid," Emmanuel said, thumping his own chest, "he's had it." It was true. René was usually quiet and serious. Though he was not particularly thin, his eyes glittered. Just now another customer was explaining to him that "with time and patience, TB can be cured." René nodded and answered solemnly between bites. Mersault walked over to the counter and ordered coffee, leaning on his elbows. The other customer went on: "Did you ever know Jean Perez? He worked for the gas company. He's dead now. He had this one bad lung. But he wanted to get out of the hospital and go home. His wife was there, see. She was nothing but his horse. You know, his sickness made him like that— he was always on top of her. She wouldn't want it, but he had to. So two, three times, every day of the week—it ends up killing a sick man." René stopped eating, a piece of bread between his teeth, and stared at the man. "Yes," he said finally, "the thing comes on fast, but it takes time to get rid of it." Mersault wrote his name with one finger on the steamed-over percolator. He blinked his eyes. Every day his life alternated between this calm consumptive and Emmanuel bursting into song, between the smell of coffee and the smell of tar, alienated from himself and his interests, from his heart, his truth. Things that in other circumstances would have excited him left him unmoved now, for they were simply part of his life, until the moment he was back in his room using all his strength and care to smother the flame of life that burned within him.

"What do you think, Mersault? You've been to school," Celeste said.

"Oh, cut it out," Patrice said, "you'll get over it."

"You're touchy this morning."

Mersault smiled and, leaving the restaurant, crossed the street and went upstairs to his room. The apartment was over a horse butcher's. Leaning over his balcony, he could smell blood as he read the sign: "To Man's Noblest Conquest." He stretched out on his bed, smoked a cigarette, and fell asleep.

He slept in what used to be his mother's room. They had had this little three-room apartment a long time. Now that he was alone, Mersault rented two rooms to a man he knew, a barrelmaker who lived with his sister, and he had kept the best room for himself. His mother had been fifty-six when she died. A beautiful woman, she had enjoyed—and expected to enjoy—a life of diversion, a life of pleasure. At forty, she had been stricken by a terrible disease. She had had to give up her clothes, her cosmetics, and was reduced to hospital gowns, her face deformed by terrible swellings; her swollen legs and her weakness kept her almost immobilized, and she would grope frantically around the colorless apartment she could no longer take care of, for she was half blind as well. The diabetes she had neglected had been further aggravated by her careless life. Mersault had had to abandon his studies and take a job. Until his mother's death, he had continued to read, to reflect. And for ten years, the sick woman endured that life. The suffering had lasted so long that those around her grew accustomed to her disease and forgot that she was deathly ill, that she would die. One day she died. People in the neighborhood felt sorry for Mersault. They expected a lot from the funeral. They recalled the son's deep feeling for his mother. They warned distant relatives not to mourn too much, so that Patrice would not feel his own grief too intensely. They were asked to protect him, to take care of him. But Patrice, dressed in his best and with his hat in his hand,

watched the arrangements. He walked in the procession, listened to the service, tossed his handful of
earth, and folded his hands. Only once did he look
surprised, expressing his regret that there were so
few cars for those who had attended the service.
That was all. The next day, a sign appeared in one
of the apartment windows: "For rent." Now he
lived in his mother's room. In the past, the poverty
they shared had a certain sweetness about it: when
the end of the day came and they would eat their
dinner in silence with the oil lamp between them,
there was a secret joy in such simplicity, such retrenchment. The neighborhood was a quiet one.
Mersault would stare at his mother's slack mouth
and smile. She would smile back. He would start
eating again. The lamp would smoke a little. His
mother tended it with the same exhausted gesture,
extending only her right arm, her body slumped
down in her chair. "You're not hungry any more?"
she would ask, a moment later. "No." He would
smoke, or read. If he smoked, she always said:
"Again!" If he read: "Sit closer to the lamp, you'll
ruin your eyes." But now the poverty in solitude
was misery. And when Mersault thought sadly of
the dead woman, his pity was actually for himself.
He could have found a more comfortable room,
but he clung to this apartment and its smell of poverty. Here, at least, he maintained contact with
what he had been, and in a life where he deliberately tried to expunge himself, this patient, sordid
confrontation helped him to survive his hours of

melancholy and regret. He had left on the door the frayed gray card on which his mother had written her name in blue pencil. He had kept the old brass bed with its sateen spread, and the portrait of his grandfather with his tiny beard and pale, motionless eyes. On the mantelpiece, shepherds and shepherdesses framed an old clock that had stopped and an oil lamp he almost never lit. The dreary furnishings —some rickety rattan chairs, the wardrobe with its yellowed mirror, a dressing table missing one corner —did not exist for him: habit had blurred everything. He moved through the ghost of an apartment that required no effort of him. In another room, he would have had to grow accustomed to novelty, to struggle once again. He wanted to diminish the surface he offered the world, to sleep until everything was consumed. For this purpose, the old room served him well. One window overlooked the street, the other a yard always full of laundry, and, beyond it, a few clumps of orange trees squeezed between high walls. Sometimes, on summer nights, he left the room dark and opened the window overlooking the yard and the dim trees. Out of the darkness the fragrance of orange blossoms rose into the darkness, strong and sweet, surrounding him with its delicate shawls. All night during the summer, he and his room were enclosed in that dense yet subtle perfume and it was as if, dead for days at a time, he had opened his window on life for the first time.

He wakened, his mouth full of sleep, his body

covered with sweat. It was very late. He combed his hair, ran downstairs, and jumped onto a street-car. By five past two he was in his office. He worked in a big room where the walls were covered with 414 pigeonholes into which folders were piled. The room was neither dirty nor sordid, but it suggested, at any hour of the day, a catacomb in which dead hours had putrefied. Mersault checked shipping bills, translated provision lists from English ships, and between three and four dealt with clients who wanted crates or luggage shipped. He had asked for this work, which really wasn't a part of his job. But at the start, he had found it a way of escaping into life. There were living faces, familiar encounters, and a passing breath of life in which at last he felt his own heart beating. And it allowed him to avoid the faces of the three secretaries and the supervisor, Monsieur Langlois. One of the secretaries was quite pretty and had been recently married. Another lived with her mother, and the third was a dignified and energetic old lady whom Mersault liked for her florid way of talking and her reticence about what Langlois called her "misfortunes." The supervisor would engage in peremptory arguments with old Madame Herbillon, who always emerged victorious. She despised Langlois for the sweat that pasted his trousers to his buttocks when he stood up and for the panic which seized him in the presence of the head of the firm and occasionally on the phone when he heard the name of some lawyer or even of some idiot with a *de* in front of his name. The poor man was quite unable to soften the old lady's heart or to win his way into her good graces. This afternoon he was strutting around the middle of the office. "We really get along very well together, don't we, Madame Herbillon?" Mersault was translating "vegetables," staring over his head at the lightbulb in its corrugated green cardboard shade. Across from him was a bright-colored calendar showing a religious procession in Newfoundland. Sponge, blotter, inkwell, and ruler were lined up on his desk. The windows near him looked out over huge piles of wood brought from Norway by yellow and white freighters. Mersault listened. On the other side of the wall, life had its own deep, muffled rhythm, a respiration that filled the harbor and the sea. So remote, and yet so close to him . . . The six o'clock bell released him. It was a Saturday.

Once home, he lay down on his bed and slept till dinnertime. He made himself some eggs and ate them out of the pan (with no bread; he had forgotten to buy any), then stretched out again and fell asleep at once. He awoke the next morning just before lunchtime, washed and went downstairs to eat. Back in his room he did two crossword puzzles, carefully cut out an advertisement for Kruschen Salts which he pasted into a booklet already filled with jovial grandfathers sliding down banisters. Then he washed his hands and went out onto his balcony. It was a beautiful afternoon. Yet the sidewalks were damp, the occasional passer-by in a hurry. Mersault stared after each one until he was out of sight, then attached his gaze to a new arrival within his field of vision. First came families walking together—two little boys in sailor suits, uncomfortable in their starched blouses, and a girl with a huge pink bow and black patent-leather shoes. Behind them a mother in a brown silk dress, a monstrous creature swathed in a boa, the father, more elegant, carrying a cane. In a little while it was the turn of the young men of the neighborhood, hair slicked back and red neckties, close-fitting jackets with embroidered pocket handkerchiefs, and square-toed shoes. They were on their way to the movies in the center of town, and hurried toward the streetcar, laughing very loud. Then the street grew still again. The afternoon diversions had begun. The neighborhood belonged to cats and shopkeepers. The sky, though clear, was lusterless over the ficus trees lining the road. Across from Mersault, the tobacconist brought a chair out in front of his door and straddled it, leaning his arms on the back. The streetcars that had been crowded a little while ago were almost empty. In the little café Chez Pierrot, the waiter was sweeping sawdust in the empty front room. Mersault turned his chair around, placed it like the tobacconist's, and smoked two cigarettes one after the other. He went back into his room, broke off a piece of chocolate, and returned to his balcony to eat it. Soon the sky darkened, then paled again. But the passing clouds had left a promise of rain over the street they dimmed. At five, streetcars groaned past, jammed with soccer fans from the outlying stadiums perched on the runningboards and hanging from the handrails. On the next streetcar, he could identify the players themselves by their canvas bags. They shouted and sang at the top of their lungs that their teams would never die. Several waved to Mersault. One shouted: "We did it this time!" "Yes," was all Mersault answered, nodding. Then there were more cars. Some had flowers wreathed in their bumpers and looped around their fins. Then the light faded a little more. Over the roofs the sky reddened, and with evening the streets grew lively again. The strollers returned, the tired children whining as they let themselves be dragged home. The neighborhood movie houses disgorged a crowd into the street. Mersault could tell from the violent gestures of the young men that they had seen some sort of adventure film. Those who had been to movies in the center of town appeared a little later. They were more serious: for all their laughter and teasing gestures, their eyes and their movements betrayed a kind of nostalgia for the magical lives they had just shared. They lingered in the street, coming and going. And on the sidewalk across from Mersault, two streams finally formed. One consisted of neighborhood girls, walking arm in arm, bareheaded. The young men in the other cracked jokes which made the girls laugh and look away. Older people went into the cafés or formed groups on the sidewalk which the human river flowed around as if they were islands. The streetlamps were on now, and the electric light made the first stars look faint in the night sky. An audience of one, Mersault watched the procession of people under the lights. The streetlamps made the damp sidewalks gleam, and at regular intervals the streetcars would throw reflections on shiny hair, wet lips, a smile, or a silver bracelet. Gradually the streetcars became more infrequent, and the night was already black above the trees and the lamps as the neighborhood gradually emptied and the first cat crept across the street as soon as it was deserted again. Mersault thought about dinner. His neck ached a little from leaning so long on the back of his chair. He went downstairs to buy bread and macaroni, made his dinner and ate it. Then he returned to his balcony. People were coming out again, the air had cooled. He shivered, closed his windows, and walked over to the mirror above the fireplace. Except for certain evenings when Marthe came or when he went out with her, and except for his correspondence with the girls in Tunis, his entire life lay in the yellowed image the mirror offered of a room where the filthy oil lamp stood among the bread crusts.

"Another Sunday shot," Mersault said.

3

When Mersault walked through the streets in the evening, proud as he watched the lights and shadows flicker across Marthe's face, everything seemed wonderfully simple, even his own strength and his courage. He was grateful to her for displaying in public, at his side, the beauty she offered him day after day like some delicate intoxication. An unnoticeable Marthe would have made him suffer as much as a Marthe happy in the desire of other men. He was glad to walk into the theater with her tonight, a little before the film began, when the hall was nearly full. She went in ahead of him, drawing glances of admiration, her flower-like face smiling, her beauty violent. Mersault, holding his hat in his hand, was overcome by a wonderful sense of ease, a kind of inner awareness of his own elegance. His expression grew remote and serious. He exaggerated his ceremonious manner, stepped back to let the usher pass, lowered Marthe's seat for her. And he did all this less from conceit, from ostentation, than because of the gratitude that made his heart suddenly swell, filling with love for all these people around him. If he gave the usher too big a tip, it was because he did not know how else to pay for his joy, and because he worshipped, by making this everyday gesture, a divinity whose brilliant smile glistened like oil in his gaze. During the break between films, strolling in the lobby lined with mirrors, he saw the face of his own happiness reflected there, populating the place with elegant and vibrant images—his own tall, dark figure and Marthe smiling in her bright dress. Yes, he liked his face as he saw it there, his mouth quivering around the cigarette between his lips and the apparent ardor of his deep-set eyes. But a man's beauty represents inner, functional truths: his face shows what he can do. And what is that compared to the magnificent uselessness of a woman's face? Mersault was aware of this now, delighting in his vanity and smiling at his secret demons.

Back in the theater, he remembered that when he was alone he never left his seat between films, preferring to smoke and to listen to the records played while the lights were still on. But tonight the excitement continued, and he felt that every chance of extending and renewing it was worth taking. Just as she was sitting down, however, Marthe returned the greeting of a man a few rows behind them. And Mersault, nodding in his turn, thought he noticed a faint smile on the man's lips. He sat down without noticing the hand Marthe laid on his shoulder to catch his attention; a moment earlier he would have responded to it with delight, as another proof of that power she acknowledged in him.

"Who's that?" he asked, waiting for the perfectly natural "who?" which in fact followed at once.

"You know. That man . . ."

"Oh," Marthe said. And that was all.

"Well?"

"Do you have to know?"

"No," Mersault said.

He glanced behind him: the man was staring at the back of Marthe's neck without moving a muscle of his face. He was rather good-looking, his lips very red and well shaped, but his eyes, which were set shallowly in his face, had no expression in them. Mersault felt the blood pounding in his temples. In his suddenly darkened vision, the brilliant hues of that ideal world where he had been living the last few hours were suddenly soiled. He didn't need to hear what she would say. He knew: the man had slept with Marthe. And what racked Mersault like panic was the thought of what this man might be thinking. He knew what it was, he had often thought the same thing: "Show off all you want . . ." The idea that this man was now imagining Marthe's every gesture, even her way of putting her arm over her eyes at the moment of pleasure, that he too had once tried to pull her arm away in order to watch the tumultuous surge of the dark gods in her eyes, made everything inside Mersault collapse, and tears of rage welled up under his closed eyelids while the theater bell announced that the film was about to begin. He forgot Marthe, who had been merely the pretext of his joy and was now the living body of his rage. Mersault kept his eyes closed a long time, and when he opened them again, a car was turning over on the screen, one of its wheels still spinning in complete silence, slower and slower, dragging into its persistent circle all the shame and humiliation that had been awakened in Mersault's angry heart. But a craving for certainty made him forget his dignity: "Marthe, was he ever your lover?"

"Yes," she said. "But I want to watch the picture."

That was the day Mersault began to be attached to Marthe. He had met her several months before, and he had been astonished by her beauty, her elegance. Her golden eyes and carefully made-up lips in that rather broad, regular face made her look like some painted goddess. The natural stupidity that glowed in her eyes emphasized her remote, impassive expression. In the past, whenever Mersault had spent any time with one woman, had made the first gestures of commitment, he was conscious of the disastrous fact that love and desire must be expressed in the same way, and he would think about the end of the affair before even taking her in his arms. But Marthe had appeared at a moment when Mersault was ridding himself of everything, of himself as well. A craving for freedom and independence is generated only in a man still living on hope. For Mersault, nothing mattered in those days. And the first time Marthe went limp in his arms and her features blurred as they came closer—the lips that had been as motionless as painted flowers now quivering and extended—Mersault saw in her not the future but all the force of his desire focused upon her and satisfied by this appearance, this image. The lips she offered him seemed a message from a world without passion and swollen with desire, where his heart would find satisfaction. And this seemed a miracle to him. His heart pounded with an emotion he almost took for love. And when he felt the ripe and resilient flesh under his teeth, it was as though he bit into a kind of fierce liberty, after caressing her a long time with his own lips. She became his mistress that same day. After some time, their harmony in lovemaking became perfect. But as he knew her better, she gradually lost the sense of strangeness, which he would try to revive as he pressed upon her mouth. So that Marthe, accustomed to Mersault's reserve and even coldness, had never understood why, in a crowded streetcar, he had one day asked for her lips. Bewildered, she had held up her face. And he had kissed her the way he liked to, first caressing her lips with his own and then slowly biting them. "What's come over you?" she asked him later. He had given her the smile she loved, the brief smile which answers, and he had said: "I feel like misbehaving," and had lapsed back into silence. She did not understand Patrice's vocabulary, either. After making love, at that moment when the heart drowses in the released body, filled only with the tender affection he might have felt for a winsome puppy, Mersault would smile at her and say, "Hello, image."

Marthe was a secretary. She did not love Mersault, but she was attached to him insofar as he intrigued her and flattered her. Since the day when Emmanuel, whom Mersault had introduced to her, had told her: "Mersault's a good guy, you know. He's got guts. But he doesn't talk—so people don't always realize what he's like," she regarded him with curiosity. And since his lovemaking satisfied her, she asked nothing more, adapting herself as best she could to a silent lover who made no demands and took her when she wanted to come. She was only a little uneasy about this man whose weak points she could not discover.

But that night, as they left the movie theater, she realized that something could hurt Mersault. She said nothing about it the rest of the evening, and slept in Mersault's bed. He did not touch her during the night. But from now on she used her advantage. She had already told him she had had other lovers; now she managed to find the necessary proofs.

The next day, departing from her usual practice, she came to his room after she had left her office. She found Mersault asleep and sat down at the foot of the brass bed without waking him. He was in his shirtsleeves, which exposed the white underside of his muscular brown forearms. He was breathing regularly, chest and belly rising together. Two creases between his eyebrows gave him a look of strength and stubbornness she knew very well. His hair curled around his tanned forehead, in which a vein throbbed. Exposed this way, his arms lying close to his sides, one leg bent, he looked like a solitary and obstinate god, flung sleeping into an alien world. Staring at his sleep-swollen lips, she desired him, and just then Mersault half-opened his eyes and closed them again, saying without anger: "I don't like being watched when I'm sleeping."

Marthe threw her arms around his neck and kissed him. He didn't move. "Oh, darling, another one of your moods . . ."

"Don't call me 'darling,' please. I've already asked you not to."

She stretched out beside him and stared at his profile. "You remind me of someone that way, I wonder who it is."

He pulled up his trousers and turned his back to her. Marthe frequently noticed Mersault's gestures in strangers, in film actors; he took it as a sign of his influence over her, but now this habit which had often flattered him was an irritation. She squeezed herself against his back and took all the warmth of his sleep against her body. Darkness was falling fast, and shadows soon filled the room. Somewhere in the building there were shouts, children crying, a cat mewing, the sound of a door slamming. The streetlamps came on, flooding the balcony. Streetcars went by only occasionally. And then the neighborhood smell of anisette and roasting meat rose in heavy gusts from the street into the room.

Marthe felt sleepy. "You're mad at me, aren't you? It started yesterday . . . that's why I came. Aren't you going to talk to me?" She shook him.

Mersault didn't move, his eyes tracing the curve of light on a shoe under the dressing table: it was already dark in the room. "You know that man yesterday? Well, I was just kidding. He was never my lover."

"No?"

"Well, not really."

Mersault said nothing. He could see the gestures so clearly, the smiles . . . He clenched his teeth. Then he got up, opened the windows, and sat down again on the bed. Marthe pressed against him, thrust her hand between two buttons of his shirt and caressed his nipples. "How many lovers have you had?" he said finally.

"Don't be like that."

Mersault said nothing.

"Maybe ten," she said.

With Mersault sleepiness always called for a cigarette. "Do I know them?" he asked as he took one out. All he could see now was a white patch where Marthe's face was. "It's the same as when we make love," he realized.

"Some of them. Around here." She rubbed her face against his shoulder and spoke in that little girl's voice she used to make Mersault treat her gently.

"Now listen to me," he said, lighting a cigarette. "Try to understand what I'm saying. Promise to tell me their names. And I want you to promise to point out the others—the ones I don't know—if we pass them in the street."

Marthe pulled away. "Oh no!"

A car sounded its horn right under the windows, then again, then twice more—long, fierce blasts. A streetcar bell sounded somewhere in the night. On the marble top of the dressing table, the alarm clock ticked coldly. Mersault spoke with deliberation: "I'm asking you to tell me because I know myself. If I don't find out exactly who they are, each man I meet will make the same thing happen—I'll wonder, I'll imagine. That's what it is, I'll imagine too much. I don't know if you understand . . ."

She understood, amazingly. She told him the names. There was only one he didn't recognize. The last she named was a man he knew, and this was the one he thought about, because he was handsome and the women ran after him. What astonished him about lovemaking was—the first time, at least—the terrible intimacy the woman accepted and the fact that she could receive a part of a stranger's body inside her own. In such intoxication and abandonment, in such surrender he recognized the exalting and sordid power of love. And it was this intimacy that was the first thing he imagined between Marthe and her lover. Just then she sat up on the edge of his bed and putting her left foot on her right thigh, took off one shoe, then the other, dropping them next to the bed so that one was lying on its side, the other standing on its high heel. Mersault felt his throat tighten. Something was gnawing at his stomach.

"Is this the way you do it with René?" he said smiling.

Marthe looked up. "Don't get any funny ideas," she said. "We only did it once."

"Oh."

"Besides, I didn't even take my shoes off."

Mersault stood up. He saw her lying back, all her clothes on, on a bed like this one, and surrendering everything, unreservedly. He shouted, "Shut up!" and walked over to the balcony.

"Oh darling!" Marthe said, sitting on the bed, her stocking feet on the floor.

Mersault controlled himself by watching the streetlamps glitter on the tracks. He had never felt so close to Marthe. And realizing that at the same time he was letting her come a little closer to him, he felt pride making his eyes sting. He walked back to her and pinched the warm skin of her neck under one ear. He smiled. "And that Zagreus—who's he? He's the only one I don't know."

"Oh him," Marthe said with a laugh, "I still see him." Mersault pinched harder. "He was the first one, you have to understand that. I was just a kid. He was older. Now he's had both legs amputated. He lives all alone. So I go see him sometimes. He's a nice man, and educated. He still reads all the time— in those days he was a student. He's always making jokes. A character. Besides, he says the same thing you do. He tells me: 'Come here, image.'"

Mersault was thinking. He let go of Marthe, and she fell back on the bed, closing her eyes. After a moment he sat down beside her and bent over her parted lips, seeking the signs of her animal divinity and the way to forget a suffering he considered unworthy. But he did nothing more than kiss her.

As he walked Marthe home, she talked about Zagreus: "I've told him about you. I told him my darling was very handsome and very strong. Then he said he'd like to meet you. Because—this is what he said: 'The sight of a good body helps me breathe.' "

"Sounds pretty crazy."

Marthe wanted to please him, and made up her mind this was the moment to stage the little scene of jealousy she had been planning, having decided she owed it to him somehow. "Oh, not so crazy as some of your friends."

"What friends?" Mersault asked, genuinely startled.

"Those little grinds . . ."

The little grinds were Rose and Claire, students in Tunis whom Mersault used to know and with whom he maintained the only correspondence in his life. He smiled and laid his hand on the nape of Marthe's neck. They walked a long time. Marthe lived near the parade grounds. Lights shone in all the upper windows of the long street, although the dark, shuttered shopwindows had a forbidding look.

"Listen, darling, you don't happen to be in love with those little grinds by any chance, do you?"

"No."

They walked on, Mersault's hand on Marthe's neck covered by the warmth of her hair.

"Do you love me?" Marthe asked suddenly.

Mersault burst out laughing. "Now that's a serious question."

"Answer me!"

"People don't love each other at our age, Marthe —they please each other, that's all. Later on, when you're old and impotent, you can love someone. At our age, you just think you do. That's all it is."

Marthe seemed sad, but he kissed her. "Goodnight, darling," she said. Mersault walked home through the dark streets. He walked quickly, aware of how the muscles in his thighs played against the smooth material of his trousers, and he thought of Zagreus and his amputated legs. He wanted to meet him, and decided to ask Marthe to introduce them.

The first time Mersault saw Zagreus, he was annoyed. Yet Zagreus had tried to avoid anything that might be embarrassing about two lovers of the same woman meeting in her presence. To do so, he had attempted to make Mersault his accomplice by calling Marthe a "good girl" and laughing very loud. Mersault had remained impassive. He told Marthe, as soon as they were alone, how much he had disliked the encounter.

"I don't like half-portions. It bothers me. It keeps me from thinking. And especially half-portions who brag."

"Oh you and your thinking," Marthe answered,

not understanding. "If I paid any attention to you . . ."

But later, that boyish laugh of Zagreus', which had at first annoyed him caught Mersault's attention and interest. Moreover, the obvious jealousy which had provoked Mersault's first judgment had disappeared as soon as he saw Zagreus. Once when Marthe quite innocently referred to the time she had known Zagreus, he advised her: "Don't bother. I can't be jealous of a man who doesn't have his legs any more. If I ever do think about the two of you, I see him like some kind of big worm on top of you. And it just makes me laugh. So don't bother, angel."

And after that he went back to visit Zagreus by himself. Zagreus talked a great deal and very fast, laughed, then fell silent. Mersault felt comfortable in the big room where Zagreus lived surrounded by books and Moroccan brass trays, the fire casting reflections on the withdrawn face of the Khmer Buddha on the desk. He listened to Zagreus. What he noticed about the cripple was that he thought before he spoke. Besides, the pent-up passion, the intense life animating this absurd stump of a man, was enough to attract Mersault, to produce in him something which, if he had been a little less guarded, he might have taken for friendship.

4

That Sunday afternoon, after talking and laughing a great deal, Roland Zagreus sat silent near the fire in his big wheelchair, wrapped in white blankets. Mersault was leaning against a bookshelf, staring at the sky and the landscape through the white silk curtains. He had come during a light rain and, not wanting to arrive too early, had spent an hour wandering around the countryside. The day was dark, and even without hearing the wind, Mersault could see the trees and branches writhing silently in the little valley. The silence was broken by a milk wagon, which trundled down the street past the villa in a tremendous racket of metal cans. Almost immediately the rain turned into a downpour, flooding the windowpanes. All the water like some thick oil on the panes, the faint hollow noise of the horse's hoofs—more audible now than the cart's uproar—the persistent hiss of the rain, this basket case beside the fire, and the silence of the room—everything seemed to have happened before, a dim melancholy past that flooded Mersault's heart the way the rain had soaked his shoes and the wind had pierced the thin material of his trousers. A few moments before, the falling vapor—neither a mist nor a rain—had washed his face like a light hand and laid bare his dark-circled eyes. Now he stared at the black clouds that kept pouring out of the sky, no sooner blurred than replaced. The creases in his trousers had vanished, and with them the warmth and confidence of a world made for ordinary men. He moved closer to the fire and to Zagreus and sat facing him, in the shadow of the high mantelpiece and yet within sight of the sky. Zagreus glanced at Mersault, then looked away and tossed into the fire a ball of paper he had crumpled in his left hand. The gesture, as always ridiculous, disconcerted Mersault: the sight of this mutilated body made him uneasy. Zagreus smiled but said nothing, then suddenly thrust his face toward Mersault. The flames gleamed on his left cheek only, but something in his voice and eyes was filled with warmth. "You look tired," he said.

Abashed, Mersault merely answered: "Yes, I don't know what to do," and after a pause straightened up, walked to the window, and added as he stared outside: "I feel like getting married, or committing suicide, or subscribing to *L'Illustration*. Something desperate, you know."

Zagreus smiled. "You're a poor man, Mersault. That explains half of your disgust. And the other half you owe to your own submission to poverty."

Mersault kept his back turned, staring at the trees in the wind. Zagreus smoothed the blanket over his legs.

"You know, a man always judges himself by the balance he can strike between the needs of his body and the demands of his mind. You're judging yourself now, Mersault, and you don't like the sentence.

You live badly. Like a barbarian." He turned his head toward Patrice: "You like driving a car, don't you?"

"Yes."

"You like women?"

"When they're beautiful."

"That's what I meant." Zagreus turned back to the fire. After a moment, he began: "All those things . . ." Mersault turned around, leaning against the window, which yielded slightly to his weight, and waited for the rest of the sentence. Zagreus remained silent. A fly buzzed against the glass. Mersault turned, caught it under his hand, then let it go. Zagreus watched him and said, hesitantly: "I don't like talking seriously. Because then there's only one thing to talk about—the justification you can give for your life. And I don't see how I can justify my amputated legs."

"Neither do I," Mersault said without turning around.

Zagreus' young laugh suddenly burst out. "Thanks. You don't leave me any illusions." He changed his tone: "But you're right to be hard. Still, there's something I'd like to say to you." And he broke off again. Mersault came over and sat down, facing him. "Listen," Zagreus resumed, "and look at me. I have someone to help me, to set me on the toilet, and afterwards to wash me and dry me. Worse, I pay someone for it. Yet I'll never make a move to cut short a life I believe in that much . . .

I'd accept even worse—blind, dumb, anything, as long as I feel in my belly that dark fire that is me, me alive. The only thing that would occur to me would be to thank life for letting me burn on." Zagreus flung his body back in the chair, out of breath. There was less of him to see now, only the whitish reflection the blankets left on his chin. Then he went on: "And you, Mersault, with a body like yours, your one duty is to live and be happy."

"Don't make me laugh," Mersault said. "With eight hours a day at the office. Oh, it would be different if I was free!" He grew excited as he spoke, and as occasionally happened, hope flooded him once more, even more powerfully today because of Zagreus' reassurance. He believed that at last he could confide in someone. He resisted the impulse for a moment, began to stub out a cigarette, then continued more calmly: "A few years ago I had everything before me—people talked to me about my life, about my future. And I said yes. I even did the things you had to do to have such things. But even back then, it was all alien to me. To devote myself to impersonality—that's what concerned me. Not to be happy, not to be 'against.' I can't explain it, but you know what I mean."

"Yes," Zagreus said.

"Even now, if I had the time . . . I would only have to let myself go. Everything else that would happen to me would be like rain on a stone. The stone cools off and that's fine. Another day, the sun bakes it. I've always thought that's exactly what happiness would be."

Zagreus had folded his hands. In the silence that followed, the rain seemed to come down twice as hard, and the clouds swelled in a vague mist. The room grew a little darker, as if the sky was pouring its burden of shadow and silence into it. And the cripple said intensely: "A body always has the ideal it deserves. That ideal of a stone—if I may say so, you'd have to have a demigod's body to sustain it."

"Right," Mersault said, a little surprised, "but don't exaggerate—I've done a lot of sports, that's all. And I'm capable of going quite far in pleasure."

Zagreus reflected. "Yes—so much the better for you. To know your body's limits—that's the true psychology. But it doesn't matter anyway. We don't have time to be ourselves. We only have time to be happy. But would you mind defining what you mean by impersonality?"

"No," Mersault said, but that was all.

Zagreus took a sip of tea and set down his full cup. He drank very little, preferring to urinate only once a day. He willed himself to reduce the burden of humiliations each day brought him. "You can't save a little here, a little there," he had told Mersault one day. "It's a record like any other." For the first time a few raindrops fell down the chimney. The fire hissed. The rain beat harder on the windowpanes. Somewhere a door slammed. On the road, automobiles streaked by like gleaming rats. One of them blew its horn, and across the valley the hollow, lugubrious blast made the wet space of the world even larger, until its very memory became for Mersault an element of the silence and the agony of that sky.

"I'm sorry, Zagreus, but it's been a long time since I talked about certain things. So I don't know any more—or I'm not sure. When I look at my life and its secret colors, I feel like bursting into tears. Like that sky. It's rain and sun both, noon and midnight. You know, Zagreus, I think of the lips I've kissed, and of the wretched child I was, and of the madness of life and the ambition that sometimes carries me away. I'm all those things at once. I'm sure there are times when you wouldn't even recognize me. Extreme in misery, excessive in happiness —I can't say it."

"You're playing several games at the same time?"

"Yes, but not as an amateur," Mersault said vehemently. "Each time I think of that flood of pain and joy in myself, I know—I can't tell you how deeply I know that the game I'm playing is the most serious and exciting one of all."

Zagreus smiled. "Then you have something to do?"

Mersault said vehemently: "I have my living to earn. My work—those eight hours a day other people can stand—my work keeps me from doing it." He broke off and lit the cigarette he had held till now between his fingers. "And yet," he said, the match still burning, "if I was strong enough, and patient enough . . ." He blew out the match and pressed the tip against the back of his left hand. ". . . I know what kind of life I'd have. I wouldn't make an experiment out of my life: I would *be* the experiment of my life. Yes, I know what passion would fill me with all its power. Before, I was too young. I got in the way. Now I know that acting and loving and suffering is living, of course, but it's living only insofar as you can be transparent and accept your fate, like the unique reflection of a rainbow of joys and passions which is the same for everyone."

"Yes," Zagreus said, "but you can't live that way and work . . ."

"No, because I'm constantly in revolt. That's what's wrong."

Zagreus said nothing. The rain had stopped, but in the sky night had replaced the clouds, and the darkness was now virtually complete in the room. Only the fire illuminated their gleaming faces. Zagreus, silent for a long time, stared at Patrice, and all he said was: "Anyone who loves you is in for a lot of pain . . ." and stopped, surprised when Mersault suddenly stood up.

"Other people's feelings have no hold over me," Patrice exclaimed, thrusting his head into the shadows.

"True," Zagreus said, "I was just remarking on the fact. You'll be alone someday, that's all. Now sit down and listen to me. What you've told me is interesting. One thing especially, because it confirms everything my own experience of human beings has taught me. I like you very much, Mersault. Because of your body, moreover. It's your body that's taught you all that. Today I feel as if I can talk to you frankly."

Mersault sat down again slowly, and his face turned back to the already dimmer firelight that was sinking closer to the coals. Suddenly a kind of opening in the darkness appeared in the square of the window between the silk curtains. Something relented behind the panes. A milky glow entered the room, and Mersault recognized on the Bodhisattva's ironic lips and on the cased brass of the trays the familiar and fugitive signs of the nights of moonlight and starlight he loved so much. It was as if the night had lost its lining of clouds and shone now in its tranquil luster. The cars went by more slowly. Deep in the valley, a sudden agitation readied the birds for sleep. Footsteps passed in front of the house, and in this night that covered the world like milk, every noise seemed larger, more distinct. Between the reddening fire, the ticking of the clock, and the secret life of the familiar objects which surrounded him, a fugitive poetry was being woven which prepared Mersault to receive in a different mood, in confidence and love, what Zagreus would say. He leaned back in his chair, and it was in front of the milky sky that he listened to Zagreus' strange story.

"What I'm sure of," he began, "is that you can't be happy without money. That's all. I don't like superficiality and I don't like romanticism. I like to be conscious. And what I've noticed is that there's a kind of spiritual snobbism in certain 'superior beings' who think that money isn't necessary for happiness. Which is stupid, which is false, and to a certain degree cowardly. You see, Mersault, for a man who is well born, being happy is never complicated. It's enough to take up the general fate, only not with the will for renunciation like so many fake great men, but with the will for happiness. Only it takes time to be happy. A lot of time. Happiness, too, is a long patience. And in almost every case, we use up our lives making money, when we should be using our money to gain time. That's the only problem that's ever interested me. Very specific. Very clear." Zagreus stopped talking and closed his eyes. Mersault kept on staring at the sky. For a moment the sounds of the road and the countryside became distinct, and then Zagreus went on, without hurrying: "Oh, I know perfectly well that most rich men have no sense of happiness. But that's not the question. To have money is to have time. That's my main point. Time can be bought. Everything can be bought. To be or to become rich is to have time to be happy, if you deserve it." He looked at Patrice. "At twenty-five, Mersault, I had already realized that any man with the sense, the will, and the craving for happiness was entitled to be rich. The craving for happiness seemed to me the noblest thing in man's heart. In my eyes, that justified everything. A pure heart was enough . . ." Still looking at Mersault, Zagreus suddenly began to speak more slowly, in a cold harsh tone, as if he wanted to rouse Mersault from his apparent distraction. "At twenty-five I began making my fortune. I didn't let the law get in my way. I wouldn't have let anything get in my way. In a few years, I had done it—you know what I mean, Mersault, nearly two million. The world was all before me. And with the world, the life I had dreamed of in solitude and anticipation . . ." After a pause Zagreus continued in a lower voice: "The life I would have had, Mersault, without the accident that took off my legs almost immediately afterwards. I haven't been able to stop living . . . And now, here I am. You understand —you have to understand that I didn't want to live a lesser life, a diminished life. For twenty years my money has been here, beside me. I've lived modestly. I've scarcely touched the capital." He passed his hard palms over his eyelids and said, even more softly: "Life should never be tainted with a cripple's kisses."

At this moment Zagreus had opened the chest next to the fireplace and showed Mersault a tarnished steel safe inside, the key in the lock. On top of the safe lay a white envelope and a large black revolver. Zagreus had answered Mersault's involuntarily curious stare with a smile. It was very simple. On days when the tragedy which had robbed him of

his life was too much for him, he took out this
letter, which he had not dated and which explained
his desire to die. Then he laid the gun on the table,
bent down to it and pressed his forehead against it,
rolling his temples over it, calming the fever of his
cheeks against the cold steel. For a long time he
stayed like that, letting his fingers caress the trigger,
lifting the safety catch, until the world fell silent
around him and his whole being, already half-
asleep, united with the sensation of the cold, salty
metal from which death could emerge. Realizing
then that it would be enough for him to date his
letter and pull the trigger, discovering the absurd
feasibility of death, he knew his imagination was
vivid enough to show him the full horror of what
life's negation meant for him, and he drowned in
his somnolence all his craving to live, to go on burning in dignity and silence. Then, waking completely, his mouth full of already bitter saliva, he
would lick the gun barrel, sticking his tongue into
it and sucking out an impossible happiness.

"Of course my life is ruined. But I was right in
those days: everything for happiness, against the
world which surrounds us with its violence and its
stupidity." Zagreus laughed then and added: "You
see, Mersault, all the misery and cruelty of our civilization can be measured by this one stupid axiom:
happy nations have no history."

It was very late now. Mersault could not tell
what time it was--his head throbbed with feverish

excitement. The heat and the harshness of the cigarettes he had smoked filled his mouth. Even the light
around him was an accomplice still. For the first
time since Zagreus had begun his story, he glanced
toward him: "I think I understand."

Exhausted by his long effort, the cripple was
breathing hoarsely. After a silence he nonetheless
said, laboriously: "I'd like to be sure. Don't think
I'm saying that money makes happiness. I only mean
that for a certain class of beings happiness is possible, provided they have time, and that having
money is a way of being free of money."

He had slumped down in his chair, under his
blankets. The night had closed in again, and Mersault could scarcely see Zagreus now. A long silence
followed, and Mersault, wanting to re-establish contact, to assure himself of the other man's presence
in the darkness, stood up and said, as though grop-
ing: "It's a beautiful risk to take."

"Yes," Zagreus said, almost in a whisper. "And
it's better to bet on this life than on the next. For
me, of course, it's another matter."

"A wreck," Mersault thought. "A zero in the
world."

"For twenty years I've been unable to have the
experience of a certain happiness. This life which
devours me—I won't have known it to the full,
and what frightens me about death is the certainty it
will bring me that my life has been consummated
without me. I will have lived . . . marginally—do

you understand?" With no transition, a young man's laugh emerged from the darkness: "Which means, Mersault, that underneath, and in my condition, I still have hope."

Mersault took a few steps toward the table.

"Think about it," Zagreus said, "think about it."

Mersault merely asked: "Can I turn on the light?"

"Please."

Zagreus' nostrils and his round eyes looked paler in the sudden glare. He was still breathing hard. When Mersault held out his hand he replied by shaking his head and laughing too loud. "Don't take me too seriously. It always annoys me—the tragic look that comes into people's faces when they see my stumps."

"He's playing games with me," Mersault thought.

"Don't take anything seriously except happiness. Think about it, Mersault, you have a pure heart. Think about it." Then he looked him straight in the eyes and after a pause said: "Besides, you have two legs, which doesn't do any harm." He smiled then and rang a bell. "Clear out now, it's time for peepee."

5

Walking home that Sunday evening, Mersault couldn't stop thinking about Zagreus. But as he walked up the stairs to his room, he heard groans coming from the barrelmaker Cardona's apartment. He knocked. No one answered, but the groans continued, and Mersault walked right in. The barrelmaker was huddled on his bed, sobbing like a child. At his feet was the photograph of an old woman. "She's dead," Cardona gasped. It was true, but it had happened a long time ago.

Cardona was deaf, half-dumb, a mean and violent man. Until recently he had lived with his sister, but his tyranny had at last exhausted the woman, and she had taken refuge with her children. And he had remained alone, as helpless as a man can be who must cook and clean for himself for the first time in his life. His sister had described their quarrels to Mersault one day when she had met him in the street. Cardona was thirty, short, rather handsome. Since childhood he had lived with his mother, the only human being ever to inspire him with fear—superstitious rather than justified, moreover. He had loved her with all his uncouth heart, which is to say both harshly and eagerly, and the best proof of his affection was his way of teasing the old woman by mouthing, with difficulty, the worst abuse of priests and the Church. If he had lived so long with his mother, it was also because he had never induced any other woman to care for him. Infrequent pickups in a brothel authorized him, however, to call himself a man.

The mother died. From then on, he had lived with his sister. Mersault rented them the room they occupied. Each quite solitary, they struggled through a long, dark, dirty life. They found it hard to speak to each other, they went for days without a word. But now she had left. He was too proud to complain, to ask her to come back: he lived alone. Mornings, he ate in the restaurant downstairs, evenings up in his room, bringing food from a *charcuterie*. He washed his own sheets, his overalls. But he left his room utterly filthy. Sometimes, though— soon after the sister had left him—he would start his Sundays by taking a rag and trying to clean up the place. But his man's clumsiness—a saucepan on the mantelpiece that had once been decorated with vases and figurines—showed up in the neglect in which everything was left. What he called "putting things in order" consisted of hiding the disorder, pushing dirty clothes behind cushions or arranging the most disparate objects on the sideboard. Finally he tired of making the effort, no longer bothered to make his bed, and slept with his dog on the fetid blankets. His sister had said to Mersault: "He carries on in the café, but the woman in the laundry told me she saw him crying when he had to wash his own sheets." And it was a fact that, hardened as he was, a terror seized this man at certain times and forced him to acknowledge the extent of his desolation. Of course the sister had lived with him out of pity, she had told Mersault. But Cardona kept her from seeing the man she loved. At their age, though, it didn't matter much any more. Her boyfriend was a married man. He brought her flowers he had picked in the suburban hedgerows, oranges, and tiny bottles of liqueur he had won at shooting galleries. Not that he was handsome or anything—but you can't eat good looks for dinner, and he was so decent. She valued him, and he valued her—wasn't that love? She did his laundry for him and tried to keep things nice. He used to wear a handkerchief folded in a triangle and knotted around his neck: she made his handkerchiefs very white, and that was one of his pleasures.

But her brother wouldn't let him come to the house. She had to see him on the sly. Once she had let him come, and her brother had caught them, and there had been a terrible brawl. The handkerchief folded in a triangle had been left behind, in a filthy corner of the room, and she had taken refuge with her son. Mersault thought of that handkerchief as he stared around the sordid room.

At the time, people had felt sorry for the lonely barrelmaker. He had mentioned a possible marriage to Mersault. An older woman, who had doubtless been tempted by the prospect of young, vigorous caresses . . . She had them before the wedding.

After a while her suitor abandoned the plan, declaring she was too old for him. And he was alone in this little room. Gradually the filth encircled him, besieged him, took over his bed, then submerged everything irretrievably. The place was too ugly, and for a man who doesn't like his own room, there is a more accessible one, comfortable, bright, and always welcoming: the café. In this neighborhood, the cafés were particularly lively. They gave off that herd warmth which is the last refuge against the terrors of solitude and its vague aspirations. The taciturn creature took up his residence in them. Mersault saw him in one or another every night. Thanks to the cafés, he postponed the moment of his return as long as possible. In them he regained his place among men. But tonight, no doubt, the cafés had not been enough. And on his way home, he must have taken out that photograph which wakened the echoes of a dead past. He rediscovered the woman he had loved and teased so long. In the hideous room, alone with the futility of his life, mustering his last forces, he had become conscious of the past that had once been his happiness. Or so he must have thought, at least, since at the contact of that past and his wretched present, a spark of the divine had touched him and he had begun to weep.

Now, as whenever he found himself confronting a brutal manifestation of life, Mersault was powerless, filled with respect for that animal pain. He sat down on the dirty, rumpled blankets and laid one hand on Cardona's shoulder. In front of him, on the oilcloth covering the table, was an oil lamp, a bottle of wine, crusts of bread, a piece of cheese, and a tool box. In the corners of the ceiling, festoons of cobwebs. Mersault, who had never been in this room since his own mother's death, measured the distance this man had traveled by the desolation around him. The window overlooking the courtyard was closed. The other window was open only a crack. The oil lamp, in a fixture surrounded by a tiny deck of china cards, cast its calm circle of light on the table, on Mersault's and Cardona's feet, and on a chair facing them. Meanwhile Cardona had picked up the photograph and was staring at it, kissing it, mumbling: "Poor *Maman*." But it was himself he was pitying. She was buried in the hideous cemetery Mersault knew well, on the other side of town.

He wanted to leave. Speaking slowly to make himself understood, he said: "You-can't-stay-here-like-this."

"No more work," Cardona gasped, and holding out the photograph, he stammered: "I loved her, I loved her," and Mersault translated: "She loved me." "She's dead," and Mersault understood: "I'm alone." "I made her that for her last birthday." On the mantelpiece was a tiny wooden barrel with brass hoops and a shiny spigot. Mersault let go of Cardona's shoulder, and he collapsed on the dirty pillows. From under the bed came a deep sigh and a sickening smell. The dog dragged itself out, flattening its rump, and rested its head on Mersault's lap, its long ears pricked up, its golden eyes staring into his own. Mersault looked at the little barrel. In the miserable room where there was scarcely enough air to breathe, with the dog's warmth under his fingers, he closed his eyes on the despair that rose within him like a tide for the first time in a long while. Today, in the face of abjection and solitude, his heart said: "No." And in the great distress that washed over him, Mersault realized that his rebellion was the only authentic thing in him, and that everything else was misery and submission. The street that had been so animated under his windows the day before still swelled with life. From the gardens beyond the courtyard rose a smell of grass. Mersault offered Cardona a cigarette, and both men smoked without speaking. The last streetcars passed and with them the still-vivid memories of men and lights. Cardona fell asleep and soon began snoring, his nose stuffed with tears. The dog, curling up at Mersault's feet, stirred occasionally and moaned in its dreams. Each time it moved, its smell reached Mersault, who was leaning against the wall, trying to choke down the rebellion in his heart. The lamp smoked, charred, and finally went out with a stink of oil. Mersault dozed off and awakened with his eyes fixed on the bottle of wine. Making a tremendous effort, he stood up, walked over to the rear window and stood there: out of the night's heart sounds and silences mounted toward him. At the limits of this sleeping world, a long blast from a ship summoned men to depart, to begin again.

The next morning, Mersault killed Zagreus, came home, and slept all afternoon. He awakened in a fever. That evening, still in bed, he sent for the neighborhood doctor, who told him he had grippe. A man from his office who had come to find out what was the matter took Mersault's resignation to Monsieur Langlois. A few days later, everything was settled: an article in the newspaper, an investigation. There was every motive for Zagreus' action. Marthe came to see Mersault and said with a sigh: "Sometimes there are days when you'd like to change places with him. But sometimes it takes more courage to live than to shoot yourself." A week later, Mersault boarded a ship for Marseilles. He told everyone he was going to France for a rest. From Lyons, Marthe received a letter of farewell from which only her pride suffered. In the same letter Mersault said he had been offered an exceptional job in central Europe. Marthe wrote him at a general-delivery address about how much she was suffering. Her letter never reached Mersault, who had a violent attack of fever the day after he reached Lyons, and took the first train for Prague. As it happened, Marthe told him that, after several days in the morgue, Zagreus had been buried and that it had taken a lot of pillows to wedge his body into the coffin.

Part Two

Conscious
Death

1

"I'd like a room," the man said in German.

The clerk was sitting in front of a board covered with keys and was separated from the lobby by a broad table. He stared at the man who had just come in, a gray raincoat over his shoulders, and who spoke with his head turned away. "Certainly, sir. For one night?"

"No, I don't know."

"We have rooms at eighteen, twenty-five, and thirty crowns."

Mersault looked through the glass door of the hotel out into the little Prague street, his hands in his pockets, his hair rumpled. Not far away, he could hear the streetcars screeching down the Avenue Wenceslas.

"Which room would you like, sir?"

"It doesn't matter," Mersault said, still staring through the glass door. The clerk took a key off the rack and handed it to Mersault.

"Room number twelve," he said.

Mersault seemed to wake up. "How much is this room?"

"Thirty crowns."

"That's too much. Give me a room for eighteen."

Without a word, the man took another key off the rack and indicated the brass star attached to it: "Room number thirty-four."

Sitting in his room, Mersault took off his jacket, loosened his tie, and mechanically rolled up his shirt-sleeves. He walked over to the mirror above the sink, meeting a drawn face slightly tanned where it was not darkened by several days' growth of beard. His hair fell in a tangle over his forehead, down to the two deep creases between his eyebrows, which gave him a grave, tender expression, he realized. Only then did he think of looking around this miserable room which was all the comfort he had and beyond which he envisioned nothing at all. On a sickening carpet—huge yellow flowers against a gray background—a whole geography of filth suggested a grimy universe of wretchedness. Behind the huge radiator, clots of dust; the regulator was broken, and the brass contact points were exposed. Over the sagging bed dangled a flyspecked wire, at its end a sticky lightbulb. Mersault inspected the sheets, which were clean. He took his toilet things out of the overnight bag and arranged them one by one on the sink. Then he started to wash his hands, but turned off the tap and walked over to open the uncurtained window. It overlooked a courtyard with a washing trough and a series of tiny windows in the walls. Laundry was drying on a cord stretched between two of them. Mersault lay down on the bed and fell asleep at once. He wakened with a start, sweating, his clothes rumpled, and walked aimlessly around the room. Then he lit a cigarette, sat down on the bed, and stared at the wrinkles in his trousers. The sour taste of sleep mingled with the cigarette smoke. He stared at the room again, scratching his ribs through his shirt. He was flooded by a dreadful pleasure at the prospect of so much desolation and solitude. To be so far away from everything, even from his fever, to suffer so distinctly here what was absurd and miserable in even the tidiest lives showed him the shameful and secret countenance of a kind of freedom born of the suspect, the shady. Around him the flaccid hours lapped like a stagnant pond—time had gone slack.

Someone knocked violently, and Mersault, startled, realized that he had been awakened by the same knocking. He opened the door to find a little old man with red hair bent double under Mersault's two suitcases, which looked enormous in his hands. He was choking with rage, and his wide-spaced teeth released a stream of saliva as well as insults and recriminations. Mersault remembered the broken handle, which made the larger suitcase so difficult to carry. He wanted to apologize, but had no idea how to say he had never thought the porter would be so old. The tiny creature interrupted him: "That's fourteen crowns."

"For one day's storage?" Mersault asked, surprised. Then he understood, from the old man's laborious explanations, that the porter had taken a taxi. But Mersault dared not say that he himself could also have taken a taxi in that case, and he paid out of sheer reluctance to argue. Once the door was shut, Mersault felt inexplicable sobs swelling his chest. A nearby clock chimed four times. He had slept two hours. He realized he was separated from the street only by the house opposite his window, and he felt the dim, mysterious current of life so close to him. It would be better to go outside. Mersault washed his hands very carefully. He sat down on the bed again to clean his nails, and worked the file methodically. Down in the courtyard two or three buzzers rang out so emphatically that Mersault went back to the window. He noticed that an arched passageway led through the house to the street. It was as if all the voices of the street, all the unknown life on the other side of that house, the sounds of men who have an address, a family, arguments with an uncle, preferences at dinner, chronic diseases, the swarm of beings each of whom has his own personality, forever divided from the monstrous heart of humanity by individual beats, filtered now through the passageway and rose through the courtyard to explode like bubbles in Mersault's room. Discovering how porous he was, how attentive to each sign the world made, Mersault recognized the deep flaw that opened his being to life. He lit another cigarette and hurriedly dressed. As he buttoned his jacket, the smoke stung his eyes. He turned back to the sink, put cold water on his eyes, and decided to comb his hair. But his comb had vanished. He was unable to smooth the sleep-rumpled curls with his fingers. He went downstairs as he was, his hair sticking up behind and hanging over his forehead. He felt diminished even further. Once out in the street, he walked around the hotel to reach the little passageway he had noticed. It opened onto the square of the old town hall, and in the heavy evening that sank over Prague, the Gothic steeples of the town hall and of the old Tyn church were silhouetted, black against the dim sky. Crowds of people were walking under the arcades lining the old streets. Each time a woman passed him, Mersault waited for the glance that would permit him to consider himself still capable of playing the delicate and tender game of life. But healthy people have a natural skill in avoiding feverish eyes. Unshaven, his hair rumpled, in his eyes the expression of some restless animal, his trousers as wrinkled as his shirt collar, Mersault had lost that wonderful confidence bestowed by a well-cut suit or the steering wheel of a car. The light turned coppery, and the day still lingered on the gold of the baroque domes at the far end of the square. He walked toward one of them, went into the church, and, overcome by the ancient smell, sat down on a bench. The vaults above him were quite dark, but the gilded capitals shed a mysterious golden liquid which flowed down the grooves of the columns to the puffy faces of angels and grinning saints. Peace, yes, there was peace here, but so bitter that Mersault hurried to the threshold and stood on the steps, inhaling the evening's cooler air, into which he would plummet. In another moment, he saw the first star appear, pure and unadorned, between the steeples of Tyn.

He began to look for a cheap restaurant, making his way into darker, less crowded streets. Though it had not rained during the day, the ground was damp, and Mersault had to pick his way among black puddles glimmering between the infrequent paving stones. A light rain started to fall. The busy streets could not be far away, for he could hear the newspaper vendors hawking the *Narodni Politika*. Mersault was walking in circles now, and suddenly stopped. A strange odor reached him out of the darkness. Pungent, sour, it awakened all his associations with suffering. He tasted it on his tongue, deep in his nose; even his eyes, somehow, tasted it. It was far away, then it was at the next streetcorner, between the now-opaque sky and the sticky pavement it was there, the evil spell of the nights of Prague. He advanced to meet it, and as he did so it became more real, filling him entirely, stinging his eyes until the tears came, leaving him helpless. Turning a corner, he understood: an old woman was selling cucumbers soaked in vinegar, and it was their fragrance which had assaulted Mersault. A passer-by stopped, bought a cucumber which the old woman wrapped in a piece of paper. He took a few steps, unwrapped his purchase in front of Mersault and, as he bit into the cucumber, its broken, sopping flesh released the odor even more powerfully. Mersault leaned against a post, nauseated, and for a long moment inhaled all the alien solitude the world could offer him. Then he walked away and without even thinking what he was doing entered a restaurant where an accordion was playing. He went down several steps, stopped at the foot of the stairs, and found himself in a dim cellar filled with red lights. He must have looked peculiar, for the musician played more softly, the conversations stopped, and all the diners looked in his direction. In one corner, some whores were eating together, their mouths shiny with grease. Other customers were drinking the brown, sweetish Czech beer. Many were smoking without having ordered anything at all. Mersault went over to a rather long table at which only one man was seated. Tall and slender with yellow hair, he was sprawled in his chair with his hands in his pockets and pursed his chapped lips round a matchstick already swollen with saliva, sucking it noisily or sliding it from one corner of his mouth to the other. When Mersault sat down, the man barely moved, wedged his back against the wall, shifted the match in Mersault's direction and squinted faintly. At that moment Mersault noticed a red star in his buttonhole.

Mersault ate the little he had ordered rapidly. He was not hungry. The accordionist was playing louder now, and staring fixedly at the newcomer. Twice Mersault stared back defiantly and tried to meet the man's gaze. But fever had weakened him.

The man was still staring. Suddenly one of the whores burst out laughing, the man with the red star sucked noisily on his match and produced a little bubble of saliva, and the musician, still staring at Mersault, broke off the lively dance tune he had been playing and began a slow melody heavy with the dust of centuries. At this moment the door opened and a new customer walked in. Mersault did not see, but through the open door the smell of vinegar and cucumbers pressed in upon him, immediately filling the dark cellar, mingling with the mysterious melody of the accordion, swelling the bubble of saliva on the man's matchstick, making the conversations suddenly more meaningful, as if out of the night that lay upon Prague all the significance of a miserable suffering ancient world had taken refuge in the warmth of this room, among these people. Mersault, who was eating some kind of over-sweetened compote, suddenly at the end of his endurance, felt the flaw he carried within himself yield, exposing him still more completely to pain and fever. He stood up abruptly, called to the waiter, and understanding nothing of his explanations overpaid the check, realizing that the musician's gaze was once again fixed upon him. He walked to the door, passing the accordionist, and saw that he was still staring at the place at the table Mersault had just left. Then he realized that the man was blind, walked up the steps, and, opening the door, was entirely engulfed by the omnipresent odor as he walked through the little streets into the depths of the night.

Stars glittered over the houses. He must have been near the river; he could detect its muffled powerful voice. In front of a little gate in a thick wall covered with Hebrew characters, he realized that he was in the ghetto. Over the wall stretched the branches of a sweet-smelling willow. Through the gate he could make out big brown stones lying among the weeds: it was the old Jewish cemetery of Prague. A moment later Mersault realized he had been running and was now in the square of the old town hall. Near his hotel he had to lean against a wall and vomit, retching painfully. With all the lucidity extreme weakness affords, he managed to reach his room without making any mistakes, went to bed, and fell asleep at once.

The next day he was awakened by the newspaper vendors. The day was still overcast, but the sun glowed behind the clouds. Though still a little weak, Mersault felt better. But he thought of the long day which lay ahead of him. Living this way, in his own presence, time took on its most extreme dimensions, and each hour seemed to contain a world. The important thing was to avoid crises like the one yesterday. It would be best to do his sightseeing methodically. He sat at the table in his pajamas and worked out a systematic schedule which would occupy each of his days for a week. Monasteries and baroque churches, museums and the old parts of the city,

nothing was omitted. Then he washed, realized he
had forgotten to buy a comb, and went downstairs
as he had the day before, unkempt and taciturn, past
the clerk whose bristling hair, bewildered expression, and jacket with the second button missing he
noticed now, in broad daylight. As he left the hotel
he was brought to a halt by a childish, sentimental
accordion tune. The blind man of the night before,
squatting on his heels at the corner of the old square,
was playing with the same blank and smiling expression, as though liberated from himself and entirely
contained within the motion of a life which ex-
ceeded him. Mersault turned the corner and again
recognized the smell of cucumbers. And with the
smell, his suffering.

That day was the same as those which followed.
Mersault got up late, visited monasteries and
churches, sought refuge in their fragrance of crypts
and incense, and then, back in the daylight, confronted his secret fears at every corner, where a
cucumber vendor was invariably posted. It was
through this odor that he saw the museums and discovered the mystery and the profusion of baroque
genius which filled Prague with its gold magnifi-
cence. The altars, which glowed softly in the darkness, seemed borrowed from the coppery sky, the
misty sunlight so frequent over the city. The glistening scrolls and spirals, the elaborate setting that
looked as if it were cut out of gold paper, so touching in its resemblance to the crèches made for chil-

dren at Christmas, the grandiose and grotesque baroque perspectives affected Mersault as a kind of infantile, feverish, and overblown romanticism by which men protect themselves against their own demons. The god worshipped here was the god man fears and honors, not the god who laughs with man before the warm frolic of sea and sun. Emerging from the faint fragrance of dust and extinction which reigned under the dim vaults, Mersault felt he had no country. Every evening he visited the cloister of the Czech monks, on the west side of the city. In the cloister garden the hours fluttered away with the doves, the bells chimed softly over the grass, but it was still his fever which spoke to Mersault. Nonetheless, the time passed. But then came the hour when the churches and monuments closed and the restaurants had not yet opened. That was the dangerous time. Mersault walked along the Vltava's banks, dotted with flowerbeds and bandstands, as the day came to an end. Little boats worked their way up the river from lock to lock. Mersault kept pace with them, left behind the deafening noise and rushing water of a sluice gate, gradually regained the peace and quiet of the evening, then walked on to meet a murmur which swelled to a terrible roar. At the new lock, he watched the bright little dinghies vainly trying to pass over the dam without capsizing until one of them passed the danger point and shouts rang out above the sound of the water. The rushing river with its burden of shouts and tunes, the fragrance of gardens, full of the coppery glow of the setting sun and the twisted, grotesque shadows of the statues on the Charles Bridge, made Mersault bitterly conscious of his desolation: a solitude in which love had no part. Coming to a standstill as the fragrance of leaves and water reached him, he felt a catch in his throat and imagined tears which did not come. Tears would be for a friend, or for open arms. But tears gave way to the world without tenderness in which he was immersed. Some evenings, always at the same times, he crossed the Charles Bridge and strolled through the Hradčany district above the river, a deserted and silent neighborhood, though only a few steps from the busiest streets in the city. He wandered among these huge palaces, across enormous paved courtyards, past ironwork gates, around the cathedral. His footsteps echoed in the silence between high walls. A dim noise from the city reached him here. There was no cucumber vendor in this district, but something oppressive in the silence, in the grandeur of the place, so that Mersault always ended by walking back toward the odor or the melody which henceforth constituted his only country. He ate his meals in the restaurant he had discovered, for at least it remained familiar. He had his place beside the man with the red star, who came only in the evenings, drank a beer, and chewed on his matchstick. At dinner, too, the blind man played his accordion, and Mersault ate quickly,

paid his check, and returned to his hotel and the un-
failing sleep of a feverish child.

Every day he thought of leaving and every day,
sinking a little deeper into desolation, his longing
for happiness had a little less hold over him. He had
been in Prague four days now, and he had not yet
bought the comb whose absence he discovered each
morning. Yet he had the vague sense of something
missing, and this was what he irresolutely waited
for. One evening, he walked toward his restaurant
down the little street where he had first smelled
the cucumbers. Already he anticipated that odor,
when just before he reached the restaurant, on the
sidewalk opposite him, something made him stop,
then come closer. A man was lying there, arms
folded, head fallen on the left cheek. Three or four
people were standing against the wall, apparently
waiting for something, though very calm. One was
smoking, the others were speaking in low voices.
But one man in shirtsleeves, his jacket over his arm,
hat pushed back on his head, was performing a kind
of wild dance around the body, his gestures em-
phatic and disturbing. Overhead, the faint light of a
distant streetlamp mingled with the glow from the
nearby restaurant. The man tirelessly dancing, the
body with its folded arms, the calm spectators, the
ironic contrast and the inexplicable silence—here at
last, combining contemplation and innocence, among
the rather oppressive interplay of light and shadow,
was a moment of equilibrium beyond which it

seemed to Mersault that everything would collapse
into madness. He came closer: the dead man's head
was lying in a pool of blood. The head was turned
so that it rested on the wound. In this remote corner
of Prague, between the faint light on the moist pavement, the long wet hiss of passing cars a few steps
away, the distant screech of occasional streetcars,
death seemed insipid yet insistent too, and it was
death's summons, its damp breath, that Mersault
sensed at the very moment he began walking away
rapidly, without turning back. Suddenly the odor,
which he had forgotten, was all around him: he
went into the restaurant and sat down at his table.
The man was there, but without his matchstick. It
seemed to Mersault that there was something dis-
traught in his eyes. He dismissed the stupid notion
that occurred to him. But everything was whirling
in his mind. Before ordering anything he jumped up
and ran to his hotel, went to his room, and threw
himself on the bed. Something sharp was throbbing
in his temples. His heart empty, his belly tight,
Mersault's rebellion exploded. Images of his life
rushed before his eyes. Something inside him
clamored for the gestures of women, for arms that
opened, and for warm lips. From the depth of the
painful nights of Prague, amid smells of vinegar and
sentimental tunes, the anguished countenance of the
old baroque world which had accompanied his fever
mounted toward him. Breathing with difficulty, seeing nothing, moving mechanically, he sat up on his

bed. The drawer of the night table was open, lined with an English newspaper in which he read a whole article. Then he stretched out on the bed again. The man's head had been lying on the wound, and three or four fingers would have fit inside that wound. Mersault stared at his hands and his fingers, and childish desires rose in his heart. An intense and secret fervor swelled within him, and it was a nostalgia for cities filled with sunlight and women, with the green evenings that close all wounds. Tears burst from his eyes. Inside him widened a great lake of solitude and silence above which ran the sad song of his deliverance.

2

In the train taking him north, Mersault stared at his hands. The train's speed turned the lowering sky into an onrush of heavy clouds. Mersault was alone in the overheated compartment—he had left suddenly in the middle of the night, and with the dark morning hours ahead of him, he let the mild landscape of Bohemia rush by, the impending rain between the tall silky poplars and the distant factory chimneys filling him with an impulse to burst into tears. Then he looked at the white plaque with its three sentences: *Nicht hinauslehnen, E pericoloso sporgersi, Il est dangereux de se pencher au-dehors.* He looked again at his hands, which lay like live, wild animals on his knees: the left one long and supple, the right thicker, muscular. He knew them, recognized them, yet they were distinct from himself, as though capable of actions in which his will had no part. One came to rest against his forehead now, pressing against the fever which throbbed in his temples. The other slid down his jacket and took out of its pocket a cigarette that he immediately discarded as soon as he became aware of an overpowering desire to vomit. His hands returned to his knees, palms cupped, where they offered Mersault the emblem of his life, indifferent once more and offered to anyone who would take it.

He traveled for two days. But now it was not an

instinct of escape which drove him on. The very monotony of the journey satisfied him. The train which was jolting him halfway across Europe suspended him between two worlds—it had taken him abroad, and would deposit him somewhere, draw him out of a life the very memory of which he wanted to erase and lead him to the threshold of a new world where desire would be king. Not for a single moment was Mersault bored. He sat in his corner, rarely disturbed by anyone, stared at his hands, then at the countryside, and reflected. He deliberately extended his trip as far as Breslau, merely rousing himself at the border to change tickets. He wanted to stay where he was, contemplating his freedom. He was tired and did not feel well enough to move; he hoarded every last fragment of his strength, his hopes, kneaded them together until he had refashioned himself and his fate as well. He loved these long nights when the train rushed along the gleaming rails, roaring through the village stations where only a clock was illuminated, the sudden stops among the clustered lights of city stations where there was no time to discover where he was before the train was already swallowed up, a golden warmth cast into the compartments and then gone. Hammers pounded on the wheels, the engine exhaled its cloud of steam, and the robot gesture of the switchman lowering his red disc hurled Mersault into the train's wild course, only his lucidity, his anxiety awake. The crossword puzzle of lights and shadows went on in the compartment, a black and gold motley: Dresden, Bautzen, Gërlitz, Lugknitz. The long lonely night ahead of him, with all the time in the world to decide on the actions of a future life, the patient struggle with the thoughts eluding him on a station siding, recaptured and pursued again, the consequences reappearing and escaping once more before the dance of wires glistening under the rain and the lights. Mersault groped for the word, the sentence that would formulate the hope in his heart, that would resolve his anxiety. In his weakened state, he needed formulas. The night and then the day passed in this obstinate struggle with the word, the image which from now on would constitute the whole tonality of his mind, the sympathetic or miserable dream of his future. He closed his eyes. It takes time to live. Like any work of art, life needs to be thought about. Mersault thought about his life and exercised his bewildered consciousness and his longing for happiness in a train compartment which was like one of those cells where a man learns to know what he is by what is more than himself.

On the morning of the second day, in the middle of a field, the train slowed down. Breslau was still hours away, and the day broke over the vast Silesian plain, a treeless sea of mud under an overcast sky sagging with rainclouds. As far as the eye could see and at regular intervals, huge black birds with glistening wings flew in flocks a few yards above the ground, incapable of rising any higher under a rain-swollen sky heavy as a tombstone. They circled in a slow, ponderous flight, and sometimes one of them would leave the flock, skim the ground, almost inseparable from it, and flap in the same lethargic flight, until it was far enough away to be silhouetted on the horizon, a black dot. Mersault wiped the steam off the glass and stared greedily through the long streaks his fingers left on the pane. Between the desolate earth and the colorless sky appeared an image of the ungrateful world in which, for the first time, he came to himself at last. On this earth, restored to the despair of innocence, a traveler lost in a primitive world, he regained contact, and with his fist pressed to his chest, his face flattened against the glass, he calculated his hunger for himself and for the certainty of the splendors dormant within him. He wanted to crush himself into that mud, to re-enter the earth by immersing himself in that clay, to stand on that limitless plain covered with dirt, stretching his arms to the sooty sponge of the sky, as though confronting the superb and despairing symbol of life itself, to affirm his solidarity with the world at its worst, to declare himself life's accomplice even in its thanklessness and its filth. Then the great impulse that had sustained him collapsed for the first time since he left Prague. Mersault pressed his tears and his lips against the cold pane. Again the glass blurred, the landscape disappeared.

A few hours later he arrived in Breslau. From a distance the city looked like a forest of factory chimneys and church steeples. At close range, it was made of brick and black stone; men in visored caps walked slowly through the streets. Mersault followed them, spent the morning in a workmen's café. A boy was playing the harmonica: tune of a sentimental stupidity which eased the soul. Mersault decided to travel south again, after buying a comb. The next day he was in Vienna. He slept a part of the day and the whole next night. When he awakened, his fever was completely gone. He stuffed himself on soft-boiled eggs and thick cream for breakfast, and feeling a little squeamish walked out into a morning speckled with sunshine and rain. Vienna was a refreshing city: there was nothing to visit. St. Stephen's Cathedral was too big, and bored him. He preferred the cafés around it, and in the evening a little dancehall near the banks of the canal. During the day he strolled along the Ring, in the luxury of the shopwindows and the elegant women. He enjoyed this frivolous and expensive decor which divides man from himself in the least natural city in the world. But the women were pretty, the flowers bright and sturdy in the gardens, and over the Ring at twilight, in the brilliant carefree crowd, Mersault stared at the futile caracole of stone horses against the red sky. It was then that he remembered his friends Rose and Claire. For the first time since Lyons, he wrote a letter. It was the overflow of his silence that he put down on paper:

Dear Children,

I'm writing from Vienna. I don't know what you're doing, but speaking for myself I'm traveling for a living. I've seen a lot of beautiful things with a heavy heart. Here in Vienna beauty has been replaced by civilization. It's a relief. I'm not looking at churches or ruins. I take walks in the Ring. And in the evening, over the theaters and the sumptuous palaces, the blind steeplechase of stone horses in the sunset fills me with a strange mixture of bitterness and delight. Mornings I eat soft-boiled eggs and thick cream. I get up late, the hotel people shower attention on me. I'm very impressed with the style of the maîtres d'hotel and stuffed with good food (oh, the cream here). There are lots of shows and the women are good-looking. The only thing missing is the sun.

What are you up to? Tell me about yourselves and describe the sun to a miserable wretch who has no roots anywhere and who remains your faithful

Patrice Mersault

That evening, having written his letter, he went back to the dancehall. He had arranged to spend the evening with Helen, one of the hostesses who knew a little French and understood his poor German. Leaving the dancehall at two in the morning he walked her home, made love efficiently, and wakened the next morning against Helen's back, disinterestedly admiring her long hips and broad shoulders. He got up without waking her, slipped the money into her shoe. As he was about to open the door, she called to him: "But darling, you've made a mistake." He returned to the bed. And he had made a mistake. Unfamiliar with Austrian currency, he had left a five-hundred shilling note instead of a hundred shillings. "No," he said smiling, "it's for you—you were wonderful." Helen's freckled face broke into a grin under her rumpled blond hair; she jumped up on the bed and kissed him on both cheeks. That kiss, doubtless the first she had given him spontaneously, kindled a spark of emotion in Mersault. He made her lie down, tucked her in, walked to the door again and looked back with a smile. "Goodbye," he said. She opened her eyes wide above the sheet that was pulled up to her nose and let him vanish without a word.

A few days later, Mersault received an answer postmarked Algiers:

Dear Patrice,

We're in Algiers. Your children would be very glad to see you again. If you have nothing to do in the world, why don't you come to Algiers—we have room for you in the House. We're all happy here. We're ashamed of it, of course, but only for appearance's sake. And because of popular prejudice. If happiness appeals to you, come and try it here. It's better than re-enlisting. We bend our brows to your paternal kisses,

Rose, Claire, Catherine

P.S. Catherine protests against the word paternal.

Catherine is living with us. If you approve, she can be your third daughter.

He decided to return to Algiers by way of Genoa. As other men need to be alone before making their crucial decisions, Mersault, poisoned by solitude and alienation, needed to withdraw into friendship and confidence, to enjoy an apparent security before choosing his life.

In the train heading across northern Italy toward Genoa, he listened to the thousand voices that lured him on, the siren songs of happiness. By the time he reached the first cypresses, springing straight up from the naked soil, he had yielded. He still felt weak, feverish. But something in him had relented. Soon, as the sun advanced through the day and the sea drew closer, under a broad sky pouring light and air over the shivering olive trees, the exultation which stirred the world joined the enthusiasms of his own heart. The noise of the train, the chatter in the crowded compartment, everything that laughed and sang around him kept time to a kind of inner dance which projected him, sitting motionless hour after hour, to the ends of the earth and at last released him, jubilant and speechless, into the deafening bustle of Genoa, the brilliant harbor echoing the brilliant sky, where desire and indolence struggled against each other until dark. He was thirsty, hungry for love, eager for pleasure. The gods who burned within him cast him into the sea, on a tiny beach at one end of the harbor, where the water

tasted of salt and tar and he swam until he forgot
his own body. Then he wandered through the nar-
row, redolent streets of the old part of the city, letting the colors claw at his eyes and the sky devour
itself above the houses, the cats sleeping among the
summer's filth flattened by the burden of the sun.
He walked along a road overlooking the entire city,
and the flickering fragrant sea rose toward him in
one long, irresistible swell. Closing his eyes, Mersault gripped the warm stone he sat on, opening
them again to stare at this city where sheer excess of
life flaunted its exultant bad taste. At noon he would
sit on the ramp leading down to the harbor and
watch the women walking up from the offices on
the docks. In sandals and bright summer dresses,
breasts bobbing, they left Mersault's tongue dry and
his heart pounding with desire, a desire in which he
recognized both a release and a justification. Evenings, he would see the same women in the streets
and follow them, the ardent animal coiled in his
loins stirring with a fierce delight. For two days he
smoldered in this inhuman exultation. On the third
day he left Genoa for Algiers.

All during the crossing, staring at the water and
the light on the water, first in the morning, then in
the middle of the day, and then in the evening, he
matched his heart against the slow pulse of the sky,
and returned to himself. He scorned the vulgarity of
certain cures. Stretched out on the deck, he realized
that there could be no question of sleeping but that

he must stay awake, must remain conscious despite friends, despite the comfort of body and soul. He had to create his happiness and his justification. And doubtless the task would be easier for him now. At the strange peace that filled him as he watched the evening suddenly freshening upon the sea, the first star slowly hardening in the sky where the light died out green to be reborn yellow, he realized that after this great tumult and this fury, what was dark and wrong within him was gone now, yielding to the clear water, transparent now, of a soul restored to kindness, to resolution. He understood. How long he had craved a woman's love! And he was not made for love. All his life—the office on the docks, his room and his nights of sleep there, the restaurant he went to, his mistress—he had pursued singlemindedly a happiness which in his heart he believed was impossible. In this he was no different from everyone else. He had played at wanting to be happy. Never had he sought happiness with a conscious and deliberate desire. Never until the day . . . And from that moment on, because of a single act calculated in utter lucidity, his life had changed and happiness seemed possible. Doubtless he had given birth to this new being in suffering— but what was that suffering compared to the degrading farce he had performed till now? He saw, for instance, that what had attached him to Marthe was vanity, not love. Even that miracle of the lips she offered him was nothing more than the delighted astonishment of a power acknowledged and awakened by the conquest. The meaning of his affair with Marthe consisted of the replacement of that initial astonishment by a certainty, the triumph of vanity over modesty. What he had loved in Marthe were those evenings when they would walk into the movie theater and men's eyes turned toward her, that moment when he offered her to the world. What he loved in her was his power and his ambition to live. Even his desire, the deepest craving of his flesh, probably derived from this initial astonishment at possessing a lovely body, at mastering and humiliating it. Now he knew he was not made for such love, but for the innocent and terrible love of the dark god he would henceforth serve.

As often happens, what was best in his life had crystallized around what was worst. Claire and her friends, Zagreus and his will to happiness had all crystallized around Marthe. He knew now that it was his own will to happiness which must make the next move. But if it was to do so, he realized that he must come to terms with time, that to have time was at once the most magnificent and the most dangerous of experiments. Idleness is fatal only to the mediocre. Most men cannot even prove they are not mediocre. He had won that right. But the proof remained to be shown, the risk to be run. Only one thing had changed. He felt free of his past, and of what he had lost. He wanted nothing now but this contraction and this enclosure inside himself, this lucid and patient fervor in the face of the world. As with warm dough that's squeezed and kneaded, all he wanted was to hold his life between his hands: the way he felt during those two long nights on the train when he would talk to himself, prepare himself to live. To lick his life like barley sugar, to shape it, sharpen it, love it at last—that was his whole passion. This presence of himself to himself—henceforth his effort would be to maintain it in the face of everything in his life, even at the cost of a solitude he knew now was so difficult to endure. He would not submit. All his violence would help him now, and at the point to which it raised him, his love would join him, like a furious passion to live.

The sea wrinkled slowly against the ship's sides. The sky filled with stars. And Mersault, in silence, felt in himself extreme and violent powers to love, to marvel at this life with its countenance of sunlight and tears, this life in its salt and hot stone—it seemed that by caressing this life, all his powers of love and despair would unite. That was his poverty, that was his sole wealth. As if by writing zero, he was starting over but with a consciousness of his powers and a lucid intoxication which urged him on in the face of his fate.

And then Algiers—the slow arrival in the morning, the dazzling cascade of the Casbah above the sea, the hills and the sky, the bay's outstretched arms, the houses among the trees and the smell, already upon him, of the docks. Then Mersault realized that not once since Vienna had he thought of Zagreus as the man he had killed with his own hands. He recognized in himself that power to forget which only children have, and geniuses, and the innocent. Innocent, overwhelmed by joy, he understood at last that he was made for happiness.

3

Patrice and Catherine are having their breakfast on the terrace, in the sun. Catherine is in her bathing suit, the Boy, as Mersault's friends call him, the Boy is in his shorts, a napkin around his neck. They are eating salted tomatoes, potato salad, honey, and huge amounts of fruit. They keep the peaches on ice, and lick the tiny drops which have congealed on the velvety skins. They also make grape juice, which they drink with their faces tipped toward the sun in order to get a tan—at least the Boy does, for he knows a suntan becomes him. "Taste the sun," Patrice said, holding out his arm to Catherine. She licked his arm. "Yes," she said, "now you." He tasted too, then stretched and stroked his ribs. Catherine sprawled on her stomach and pulled her bathing suit down to her hips. "I'm not indecent, am I?"

"No," the Boy said, not looking.

The sun streamed down, lingering over his face. The moist pores absorbed this fire which sheathed his body and put him to sleep. Catherine drowned in the sun, sighed and moaned: "Oh, it's good."

"Yes," the Boy said.

The house perched on a hilltop with a view of the bay. It was known in the neighborhood as the House of the Three Students. A steep path led up to it, beginning in olive trees and ending in olive trees. Between, a kind of landing followed a gray

wall covered with obscene figures and political slo-
gans to encourage the winded visitor. Then more
olive trees, blue patches of sky between the
branches, and the smell of the gum trees bordering
reddish fields in which purple-yellow and orange
cloths were spread out to dry. After a great deal of
sweating and panting, the visitor pushed open a
little blue gate, avoiding the bougainvillea tendrils,
and then climbed a stairway steep as a ladder but
drenched in a blue shade that already slaked his
thirst. Rose, Claire, Catherine, and the Boy called
the place the House above the World. Open to the
view on all sides, it was a kind of balloon-gondola
suspended in the brilliant sky over the motley dance
of the world. From the perfect curve of the bay far
below, a nameless energy gathered up the weeds,
the grass, and the sun, swept on the pines and the
cypresses, the dusty olive trees and the eucalyptus
to the very walls of the house. Depending on the
season, white dog roses and mimosa bloomed at the
heart of this offering, or the kind of honeysuckle
that spreads its fragrance over the walls on summer
nights. White sheets and red roofs, the sea smiling
under a sky pinned without a wrinkle from one
edge of the horizon to the other—the House above
the World trained its huge bay windows on a car-
nival of colors and lights, day and night. But in the
distance, a line of high purple mountains joined the
bay and its extreme slope and contained this intoxication within its far contour. Here no one com-

plained of the steep path or of exhaustion. Everyone had his joy to conquer, every day.

Living above the world, each discovering his own weight, seeing his face brighten and darken with the day, the night, each of the four inhabitants of the house was aware of a presence that was at once a judge and a justification among them. The world, here, became a personage, counted among those from whom advice is gladly taken, those in whom equilibrium has not killed love. They called the world to witness:

"The world and I," Patrice would say about nothing in particular, "we disapprove of you."

Catherine, for whom being naked meant ridding herself of inhibitions, took advantage of the Boy's absences to undress on the terrace. And after staying out to watch the sky's colors change, she announced at dinner with a kind of sensual pride: "I was naked in front of the world."

"Yes," Patrice said scornfully, "women naturally prefer their ideas to their sensations." Then Catherine protested: she loathed being an intellectual. And Rose and Claire in chorus: "Shut up, Catherine, you're wrong."

For it was understood that Catherine was always wrong, being the one the others were fond of in the same way. She had a sluggish, toast-colored, deliberate body and an animal instinct for what is essential. No one could decipher better than Catherine the secret language of trees, of the sea, of the wind.

"That child," Claire would say, eating incessantly, "is a force of nature."

Then they would all go outside to lie in the sun, and no one would speak. Man diminishes man's powers. The world leaves them intact. Rose, Claire, Catherine, and Patrice lived, at the windows of their house, on images and appearances, consented to a kind of game they played with each other, receiving with laughter, friendship, and affection alike, but returning to the dance of sea and sky, rediscovered the secret color of their fate and finally confronted the deepest part of themselves. Sometimes the cats came to join their masters. Gula would creep out, perpetually offended, a black question mark with green eyes, slender and delicate, suddenly seized by a fit of madness and pouncing on shadows. "It's a matter of glands," Rose said, and then she would laugh, surrendering to her laugh, her eyes squinting behind the round sunglasses under her curly hair, until Gula leaped into her lap (a special privilege), and then her fingers would wander over the glistening fur and Rose subsided, relaxed, becoming a cat with tender eyes, calming the animal with her mild and fraternal hands. For cats were Rose's escape into the world, as nakedness was Catherine's. Claire preferred Cali, the other cat, as gentle and stupid as his dirty white fur, who let himself be teased for hours at a time. And Claire, her Florentine face intent, would feel her soul swell within her. Silent and withdrawn, she was given to sudden outbursts, and had a splendid appetite. Noticing that she was gaining weight, Patrice scolded her: "You're disgusting. A lovely creature is not entitled to grow ugly."

But Rose intervened: "Please stop tormenting the child. Eat, Claire darling."

And the day turned from the rising sun to the setting sun around the hills and over the sea, inside the delicate light. They laughed, teased each other, made plans. Everyone smiled at appearances and pretended to submit to them. Patrice proceeded from the face of the world to the grave and smiling faces of the young women. Sometimes he was amazed by this universe they had created around him. Friendship and trust, sun and white houses, scarcely heeded nuances, here felicities were born intact, and he could measure their precise resonance. The House above the World, they said among themselves, was not a house of pleasure, it was a house of happiness. Patrice knew it was true when night fell and they all accepted, with the last breeze on their faces, the human and dangerous temptation to be utterly unique.

Today, after the sunbath, Catherine had gone to her office. "My dear Patrice," Rose announced, suddenly appearing, "I have some good news for you."

The Boy was conscientiously lounging on a couch in the terrace room, a detective story in his hands. "My dear Rose, I'm all ears."

"Today is your turn in the kitchen."

"Splendid," Patrice said, without moving.

Rose stuffed into her student's satchel not only the sweet peppers for her lunch but also volume three of Lavisse's boring *History*, and left. Patrice, who would be cooking lentils, loafed around the big ocher room until eleven, walking between the couches and the shelves decorated with green, yellow, and red masks, touching the beige-and-orange draperies; then he quickly boiled the lentils, put some oil in the pot, an onion to brown, a tomato, a *bouquet garni*, fussed over the stove and cursed Gula and Cali for announcing their hunger, despite the fact that Rose had explained to them yesterday, "Now you animals know it's too hot in the summer to be hungry."

Catherine arrived at a quarter to twelve, stripped off her light dress and open sandals and insisted on a shower and a nap in the sun—she would be the last at the table. And Rose would admonish her: "Catherine, you're intolerable." The water hissed in the bathroom, and Claire appeared, breathless from the climb. "Lentils? I know the best way of . . ."

"I know too: you take fresh cream . . . We've all learned our lesson, dear Claire." It is a fact that Claire's recipes always begin with fresh, thick cream.

"The Boy is absolutely right," said Rose, who had just arrived.

"Yes," the Boy agreed. "Let's sit down."

Meals are served in the kitchen, which looks like a prop room: there is even a pad to write down

Rose's good lines. Claire says: "We may be chic, but we're simple too," and eats her sausage with her fingers. Catherine comes to the table duly late, drunk with the sun, and plaintive, her eyes pale with sleep. There is not enough vitriol in her soul to do justice to her office—eight hours she subtracts from the world and her life to give to a typewriter. The girls understand, thinking of what their own lives would be with those eight hours amputated. Patrice says nothing.

"Yes," Rose says, made uneasy by any show of feelings. "Well, it's your own business. Besides, you talk about that office of yours every day. We'll forbid you to speak."

"But . . ." Catherine sighs.

"Put it to a vote. One, two, three, you're outvoted."

"You see," Claire says, as the lentils are brought on, too dry, and everyone eats in silence. When Claire does the cooking and tastes her food at the table, she always adds with a satisfied expression: "My, that's just delicious!" Patrice, who has his dignity, prefers to say nothing, until everyone bursts out laughing. This is certainly not Catherine's day, for she lectures them all about reducing her office hours and asks someone to go with her to complain.

"No," Rose says, "after all, you're the one who works."

Exasperated, the "force of nature" goes outside

and lies in the sun. But soon everyone joins her there. And absently caressing Catherine's hair, Claire decrees that what this "child" needs is a man. For it is common practice in the House above the World to settle Catherine's fate, to attribute certain needs to her, and to establish their extent and variety. Of course she points out from time to time that she's old enough, etc., but no one pays any attention. "Poor thing," Rose says, "she needs a lover."

Then everyone surrenders to the sun. Catherine, who never holds a grudge, tells the gossip about her office: how Mademoiselle Perez, the tall blonde who got married recently, had asked everyone in the office for information in order to be prepared for the ordeal, and what horrifying descriptions the salesmen had given her, and with what relief, back from her honeymoon, she had smilingly declared: "It wasn't so bad as all that." "She's thirty years old," Catherine adds, pityingly.

And Rose, objecting to these off-color stories: "All right, Catherine," she says, "we aren't just girls here."

At this time of day the mail plane passes over the city, bearing the glory of its glittering metal over land and through the heavens. It enters into the movement of the harbor, incorporates itself into the course of the world, and, suddenly abandoning its frivolities, sheers off and dives down to the sea, landing in a tremendous explosion of blue and white water. Gula and Cali lie on their sides, their tiny adder-mouths showing the pink of their palates, their bodies throbbing with lustful and obscene dreams. The sky releases its burden of sun and color. Eyes closed, Catherine takes the long fall that carries her deep into herself, down where some animal stirs gently, breathing like a god.

The next Sunday, guests have been invited. It is Claire's turn in the kitchen. Hence Rose has peeled the vegetables, set the table; Claire will put the vegetables in the pots and watch over the cooking reading in her room, occasionally emerging to glance under the lids. Since Mina, the Arab girl, has not come this morning, having lost her father for the third time this year, Rose has also cleaned the house. The first guest arrives: Eliane, whom Mersault calls the Idealist. "Why?" Eliane asks. "Because when you hear something true that upsets you, you say, 'That's true, but it's not good.'" Eliane has a good heart, and she thinks she looks like *The Man with a Glove*, though no one else does. But her room is lined with reproductions of *The Man with a Glove*. Eliane is studying something or other, and the first time she came to the House above the World, she announced that she was enchanted by the inhabitants' "lack of inhibitions." In time, she has found this less convenient. A lack of inhibition means telling her that her stories are a bore, or declaring— quite amiably—as soon as the first words are out of her mouth: "Eliane, you're an idiot."

When Eliane comes into the kitchen with Noel, the second guest and a sculptor by profession, she stumbles over Catherine, who never does anything in a normal position. Now she's lying on her back, eating grapes with one hand and stirring with the other a mayonnaise that is still thin. Rose, in a huge blue apron, is admiring Gula's perspicacity—the cat has jumped up onto the shelf to eat the dessert. "No doubt about it," Rose says blissfully, "that creature has a mind of her own."

"Yes," Catherine says, "she's outdone herself today," adding that in the morning Gula, with more of a mind than ever, had broken the little green lamp and a vase as well.

Eliane and Noel, doubtless too winded to express their disgust, decide to take a seat no one has dreamed of offering them. Claire arrives, friendly and languorous, shakes hands and tastes the bouillabaisse simmering on the stove. She decides they can start. But today Patrice is late. Then he appears and explains in great detail to Eliane that he is in a good mood because the girls in the street are so pretty. The hot season is just beginning, but already the firm bodies are beginning to be revealed by the light dresses—hence Patrice, as he testifies, is left in a devastated state, mouth dry, temples throbbing, loins hot. This insistence on detail silences Eliane. At table, a general consternation follows the first spoonfuls of bouillabaisse. Claire announces playfully: "I'm afraid the bouillabaisse tastes of burned onion."

"Oh no," Noel answers politely.

Then, to test those manners, Rose asks him to purchase for the household a certain number of useful items such as a hot-water heater, Persian carpets, and a refrigerator. When Noel replies by encouraging Rose to pray for him to win the lottery, Rose becomes quite realistic: "We might as well pray for ourselves."

The sun is hot and heavy now, which makes the iced wine all the more precious, and the fruit welcome. With the coffee, Eliane bravely changes the subject to love. If she were in love, she would get married. Catherine tells her that it's more urgent when in love to make love, and that materialistic point of view convulses Eliane. Rose, the pragmatist, would approve "if unfortunately experience did not show that marriage dissolves love."

But Eliane and Catherine force their opinions into opposition and become unfair, as anyone with spirit feels obliged to do. Noel, who thinks in shapes and in clay, believes in Woman, in children, and in the patriarchal truth of a concrete and sensuous life. Then Rose, exasperated beyond endurance by the outcry raised by Eliane and Catherine, pretends to understand, suddenly, the reasons for Noel's frequent visits.

"I want to thank you now," she says, "though I find it difficult to tell you how much this discovery overwhelms me. I'll speak to my father tomorrow about 'our' project, and you yourself may apply to him in a few days."

"But . . ." Noel says, for Noel doesn't quite follow.

"Oh," Rose says, with tremendous energy, "I know. I understand without your having to speak a word: you're the kind of man who can hold his tongue and let other people guess what he's thinking. But I'm glad you've declared yourself at last, for the persistence of your attentions was beginning to sully the purity of my reputation."

Noel, vaguely amused, and also vaguely alarmed, declares himself delighted to find his aspirations crowned with success.

"Not to mention," Patrice says, before lighting a cigarette, "that you'll have to act fast. Rose's condition obliges you to take certain steps promptly."

"What?"

"Oh heavens," Claire says, "it's only her second month."

"Besides," Rose adds tenderly and persuasively, "you've reached the age when you enjoy finding your own face in another man's child."

Noel frowns, and Claire says good-naturedly: "It's only a joke. Just play along with it, Noel, and let's go inside."

At which point the discussion of principles comes to an end. Nonetheless, Rose, who does her good deeds in secret, speaks affectionately to Eliane. In the big room, Patrice sits at the window, Claire leans against the table, and Catherine is lying on the floor. The others are on the couch. There is a heavy mist over the city and the harbor, but the tugboats go about their work, and their deep hoots rise to the house on gusts of tar and fish, the world of black and red hulls, of rusty anchors and chains sticky with seaweed wakening down below. As always, the strong, fraternal summons of a life of manly effort tempts everyone. Eliane says to Rose sadly: "Then you're just like me."

"No," Rose answers, "I'm merely trying to be happy—as happy as possible."

"And love isn't the only way," Patrice says, without turning around. He is very fond of Eliane, and afraid he has hurt her feelings just now. But he understands Rose and her thirst for happiness.

"A mediocre ideal," Eliane declares.

"I don't know if it's mediocre, but it's a healthy one. And that . . ." Patrice breaks off. Rose closes her eyes. Gula has jumped into her lap, and by slowly caressing the cat's skull and back, Rose anticipates that secret marriage in which the squinting cat and the motionless woman will see the same universe out of the same half-closed eyes. Everyone muses, between the long calls of the tugboats. Rose lets Gula's purring rise within her, starting from the coiled beast in the hollow of her body. The heat presses on her eyes and immerses her in a silence inhabited by the throbbing of her own blood. The cats sleep for days at a time and make love from the first star until dawn. Their pleasures are fierce, and their sleep impenetrable. And they know that the body has a soul in which the soul has no part. "Yes," Rose says, opening her eyes, "to be as happy as possible."

Mersault was thinking about Lucienne Raynal. When he had said that the women in the streets were pretty, he meant that one woman in particular was pretty. He had met her at a friend's house. A week before they had gone out together, and having nothing to do, had strolled along the harbor boulevards, all one fine hot morning. Lucienne had not opened her mouth, and as he walked her home Mersault was startled to find himself squeezing her hand a long time and smiling at her. She was quite tall and was wearing no hat—only a white linen dress and sandals. On the boulevards they had walked into a slight breeze, and Lucienne set her feet flat on the warm cobbles, bracing herself with each step against the wind. As she did so, her dress became pasted against her body, outlining her smooth, curving belly. With her blond hair pulled back, her small straight nose, and the splendid thrust of her breasts, she represented and even sanctioned a kind of secret agreement which linked her to the earth and organized the world around her movements. As her bag swayed from her right wrist and a silver bracelet tinkled against its clasp, she raised her left hand over her head to protect herself from the sun; the tip of her right foot was still on the earth but was about to take off—and at that moment she seemed to Patrice to wed her gestures to the world.

It was then that he experienced the mysterious harmony which matched his gestures with Lucienne's . . . They walked well together, and it was no effort for him to keep in step with her. Doubtless this harmony was facilitated by Lucienne's flat shoes. But all the same, there was something in their respective strides, which were similar in both length and flexibility. Mersault noticed Lucienne's silence and the closed expression of her face; he decided she was probably not very intelligent, and that pleased him. There is something divine in mindless beauty, and Mersault was particularly responsive to it. All of this made him linger over Lucienne's hand when he said goodbye, and made him see her again, inviting her to take long walks at the same silent pace, offering their tanned faces to the sun or the stars, swimming together and matching their gestures and their strides without exchanging anything but the presence of their bodies. And then last night, Mersault had discovered again a familiar and overwhelming miracle on Lucienne's lips. Until then what moved him had been her way of clinging to his clothes, of following him, of taking his arm—her abandonment and her trust that touched him as a man. Her silence, too, by which she put all of herself into each momentary gesture and emphasized her resemblance to the cats, a resemblance to which she already owed the gravity characterizing all her actions. Yesterday, after dinner, they had strolled together on the docks. They had stopped against the ramp leading up to the boulevard, and Lucienne had pressed against Mersault. In the darkness, he felt under his fingers the cool prominent cheekbones and the warm lips which opened under his pressure. Then there was something like a great cry within him, gratuitous yet ardent. From the starry night and the city that was like a spilled sky, swollen with human lights under the warm, deep breeze that rose from the harbor, he drew the thirst of this warm spring, the limitless longing to seize from these vibrant lips all the meaning of that inhuman and dormant world, like a silence enclosed in her mouth. He bent over her, and it was as if he had rested his lips on a bird. Lucienne moaned. He nibbled her lips, and sucked in that warmth which transported him as if he had embraced the world in his arms. And she clung to him like a drowning girl, rising again and again from the depth into which she had sunk, drew back and then offered him her lips again, falling once more into the cold abyss that enfolded her like a divine oblivion.

. . . But Eliane was leaving now. A long afternoon of silence and reflection lay ahead of Mersault in his room. At dinner, no one spoke. But by mutual consent they went out onto the terrace. The days always ended by melting into the days: from the morning above the harbor, glistening with sun and mist, to the mildness of the evening above the harbor. Day broke over the sea and the sun set behind the hills, for the sky showed only the one road, passing from the sea to the hills. The world says only one thing, it wakens, then it wearies. But there always comes a time when it vanquishes by mere repetition and gains the reward of its own perseverance. Thus the days of the House above the World, woven of that luxuriant fabric of laughter and simple acts, ended on the terrace under the star-studded night. Rose and Claire and Patrice stretched out on the deckchairs, Catherine sat on the parapet.

In the sky, night showed them its shining face, radiant and secret. Lights passed far below in the harbor, and the screech of trains occasionally reached them. The stars swelled, then shrank, vanished and were reborn, drawing evanescent figures, creating new ones moment by moment. In the silence, the night recovered its density, its flesh. Filled with twinkling stars, it left in their eyes the play of lights that tears can bring. And each of them, plunging into the depths of the sky, found that extreme point where everything coincides, the secret and tender meditation which makes up the solitude of one's life.

Catherine, suddenly choked with love, could only sigh. Patrice, who felt that his voice would crack, nonetheless asked: "Don't you feel cold?"

"No," Rose said. "Besides, it's so beautiful."

Claire stood up, put her hands on the parapet and held her face up to the sky. Facing everything noble and elementary in the world, she united her life with her longing for life, identified her hopes with the movement of the stars. Suddenly turning around, she said to Patrice: "On good days, if you trust life, life has to answer you."

"Yes," Patrice said, without looking at her. A star fell. Behind it a distant beacon broadened in the night that was deeper now. Some men were climbing up the path in silence. He could hear the sound of their footsteps, their heavy breathing. Then the smell of flowers reached him.

The world always says the same thing. And in that patient truth which proceeds from star to star is established a freedom that releases us from ourselves and from others, as in that other patient truth which proceeds from death to death. Patrice, Catherine, Rose, and Claire then grew aware of the happiness born of their abandonment to the world. If this night was in some sense the figure of their fate, they marveled that it should be at once so carnal and so secret, that upon its countenance mingled both tears and the sun. And with pain and joy, their hearts learned to hear that double lesson which leads to a happy death.

It is late now. Already midnight. On the brow of this night which is like the repose and the reflection of the world, a dim surge and murmur of stars heralds the coming dawn. A tremulous light descends from the sky. Patrice looks at his friends: Catherine sitting on the parapet, her head tipped back; Rose huddled on the deckchair, her hands resting on Gula; Claire standing stiff against the parapet, her high, round forehead a white patch in the darkness. Young creatures capable of happiness, who exchange their youth and keep their secrets. He stands beside Catherine and stares over her glistening shoulder into the bowl of the sky. Rose comes over to the parapet, and all four are facing the World now. It is as if the suddenly cooler dew of the night were rinsing the signs of solitude from them, delivering them from themselves, and by that tremulous and fugitive baptism restoring them to the world. At this moment, when the night overflows with stars, their gestures are fixed against the great mute face of the sky. Patrice raises an arm toward the night, sweeping sheaves of stars in his gesture, the sea of the heavens stirred by his arm and all Algiers at his feet, around them like a dark, glittering cape of jewels and shells.

4

Early in the morning, the fog lights of Mersault's car were gleaming along the coast road. Leaving Algiers, he passed milk carts, and the warm smell of the horses made him even more aware of the morning's freshness. It was still dark. A last star dissolved slowly in the sky, and on the pale road he could hear only the motor's contented purr and occasionally, in the distance, the sound of hooves, the clatter of milk cans, until, out of the dark, his lights flashed on the shining iron of the horseshoes. Then everything vanished in the sound of speed. He was driving faster now, and the night swiftly veered to day.

Out of the darkness still retained between the hills, the car climbed an empty road overlooking the sea, where the morning declared itself. Mersault stepped on the gas. The tiny sucking sound of the wheels grew louder on the dewy pavement. At each of the many turns, Mersault's brakes made the tires squeal, and as the road straightened, the sound of the motor gaining speed momentarily drowned out the soft voices of the sea rising from the beaches below. Only an airplane permits man a more apparent solitude than the kind he discovers in an automobile. Utterly confident of his own presence, satisfied with the precision of his gestures, Mersault could at the same time return to himself and to what concerned

him. The day lay open, now, at the end of the road.
The sun rose over the sea, awakening the fields on
either side of the road, still deserted a moment before, filling them with the red fluttering of birds and
insects. Sometimes a farmer would cross one of
these fields, and Mersault, rushing past, retained no
more than the image of a figure with a sack bending
over the moist, clinging soil. Again and again the
car brought him to the edge of slopes overlooking
the sea; they grew steeper and their outline, barely
suggested in the light of dawn, grew more distinct
now, suddenly revealing prospects of olive trees,
pines, and whitewashed cottages. Then another turn
hurled the car toward the sea, which tipped up toward Mersault like an offering glowing with salt
and sleep. Then the car hissed on the pavement and
turned back toward other hillsides and the unchang-
ing sea.

A month before, Mersault had announced his departure to the House above the World. He would
travel again, then settle down somewhere around
Algiers. Several weeks later he was back, convinced
that travel now meant an alien way of life to him:
wandering seemed no more than the happiness of an
anxious man. And deep inside himself he felt a dim
exhaustion. He was eager to carry out his plan of
buying a little house somewhere in the Chenoua, between the sea and the mountains, a few kilometers
from the ruins of Tipasa. When he arrived in Algiers, he had envisioned the setting of his life. He

had made a large investment in German pharmaceuticals, paid a broker to manage his holdings for him, and thereby justified his absences from Algiers and the independent life he was leading. The investment, moreover, was more or less profitable, and he made up for his occasional losses, offering without remorse this tribute to his profound freedom. The world is always satisfied, it turns out, with a countenance it can understand. Indolence and cowardice do the rest. Independence is earned by a few words of cheap confidence. Mersault then concerned himself with Lucienne's fate.

She had no family, lived alone, worked as a secretary for a coal company, ate little but fruit, and did Swedish exercises. Mersault lent her books which she returned without a word. To his questions, she replied: "Yes, I liked it," or else: "It was a little sad." The day he decided to leave Algiers, he suggested that she live with him but continue to keep her apartment in Algiers without working, joining him when he sent for her. He proposed this with enough conviction for Lucienne to find nothing humiliating in the offer, and in fact there was nothing humiliating in it. Lucienne often realized through her body what her mind could not understand; she agreed. Mersault added: "If you want, I can marry you. But I don't see the point."

"Whatever you prefer," Lucienne said. A week later he married her and made ready to leave the city. Meanwhile Lucienne bought an orange canoe to skim over the blue sea.

Mersault twisted the wheel to avoid a venture-some hen. He was thinking of the conversation he had had with Catherine, the day he had left the House above the World—he had spent the night alone in a hotel.

It was early in the afternoon, and because it had rained that morning, the whole bay was like a wet pane of glass, the sky utterly blank above it. The cape at the opposite end of the bay stood out won-derfully clear, and lay, gilded by a sunbeam, like a huge summer snake upon the sea. Patrice had fin-ished packing and now, his arms leaning on the sill, he stared greedily at this new birth of the world.

"But if you're happy here, why are you leaving?" Catherine had asked.

"There's the risk of being loved, little Catherine, and that would keep me from being happy." Coiled on the couch, her head down, Catherine stared at Patrice. Without turning around he said: "A lot of men complicate their lives and invent problems for themselves. In my case, it's quite simple. Look . . ." He spoke facing the world, and Catherine felt for-gotten. She looked at Patrice's long fingers on the sill, studied his way of resting his weight on one hip, and without even seeing his eyes she knew how ab-sorbed his gaze would be.

"What I . . ." but she broke off, still staring at Patrice.

Small sails began riding out to sea, taking advan-tage of the calm. They approached the channel, filled it with fluttering wings, and suddenly sped outward, leaving a wake of air and water that widened in long foamy trails. From where she sat, Catherine watched them make their way out to sea, rising around Patrice like a flight of white birds. He seemed to feel the weight of her silence and her stare, turned around, took her hands and brought them close to his own body. "Never give up, Catherine. You have so much inside you, and the noblest sense of happiness of all. Don't just wait for a man to come along. That's the mistake so many women make. Find your happiness in yourself."

"I'm not complaining, Mersault," Catherine said softly, putting one hand on Patrice's shoulder. "The only thing that matters now is that you take good care of yourself." He realized then how easily his certainty could be shaken. His heart was strangely hard.

"You shouldn't have said that just now." He picked up his suitcase and went down the steep stairs, then down the path from the olive trees to the olive trees. There was nothing ahead of him now except the Chenoua, a forest of ruins and wormwood, a love without hope or despair, and the memory of a life of vinegar and flowers. He turned around. Up above, Catherine was watching him leave, motionless.

In a little less than two hours, Mersault was in sight of the Chenoua. The night's last violet shadows still lingered on the slopes that plunged into the sea, while the peak glowed in the red and yellow sunlight. There was a kind of vigorous and massive assertion of the earth here, thrusting up from the Sahel and silhouetted on the horizon, ending in this enormous bestial back that plummeted straight down into the sea. The house Mersault had bought stood on the last slopes, a hundred yards from the water already turning golden in the heat. There was only one story above the ground floor, and only one room in it, but this room was enormous and overlooked the front garden and the sea through a splendid bay window opening onto a terrace as well. Mersault hurried up to it: the sea was already forming scarves of mist, and its blue darkened while the warm red of the terrace tiles glistened in the morning dew. The whitewashed parapet had already been conquered by the first tendrils of a triumphant rambler rose. The firm white flesh of the open petals, sharp against the sea, was both voluptuous and satiating. Downstairs, one room faced the foothills of the Chenoua, covered with fruit trees, the other two opened onto the garden and the sea beyond. In the garden, two pines thrust their bare trunks high into the sky, the tips alone covered with a green and yellow pelt. From the house he could see only the space bracketed between these two trees, the curve of beach between the trunks. A little steamboat was moving out to sea now, and Mersault watched its entire trajectory from one pine to the other.

Here was where he would live. Doubtless because the beauty of the place touched his heart—why else had he bought this house? But the release he hoped to find here dismayed him, this solitude he had sought so deliberately seemed even more disturbing, now that he knew its setting. The village was not far away, a few hundred yards. He walked out of the house. A little path sloped down from the road toward the sea. Following it, he noticed for the first time that he could glimpse, across the bay, the slender peninsula of Tipasa. At its very end were silhouetted the golden columns of the temple and around them the fallen ruins among the wormwood bushes forming, at this distance, a blue-gray plumage. On June evenings, Mersault reflected, the wind would bring the fragrance of those sun-gorged shrubs across the water toward the Chenoua.

He had to set up his house, organize his life. The first days passed quickly. He whitewashed the walls, bought hangings in Algiers, began to install electricity, and as he went about his work, interrupted by the meals he took at the village café and by his dips in the sea, he forgot why he had come here and lost himself in his body's fatigue, loins aching and legs stiff, fretting over the shortage of paint or the defective installation of a light fixture in the hallway. He slept at the hotel and gradually became acquainted with the village: the boys who came to play pool and ping-pong on Sunday afternoons (they would use the table all afternoon, taking only one drink, to the owner's great annoyance); the girls who strolled in the evening along the road overlooking the sea (they walked arm in arm, and there was a caressing, singsong note in their voices); Perez, the fisherman who supplied the hotel with fish and had only one arm. Here, too, he met the village doctor, Bernard. But the day the house was entirely ready, Mersault moved all his things into it and gradually recovered himself. It was evening. He was in the big room upstairs, and behind the window two worlds fought for the space between the two pines. In one, almost transparent, the stars multiplied. In the other, denser and darker, a secret palpitation of the water betrayed the sea.

So far, he had lived sociably enough, chatting with the workmen who helped him in the house or with the owner of the café. But now he realized that he had no one to meet tonight, nor tomorrow, nor ever, and that he was facing his longed-for solitude at last. From the moment he no longer had to see anyone, the next day seemed terribly imminent. Yet he convinced himself that this was what he had wanted: nothing before him but himself for a long time—until the end. He decided to stay where he was, smoking and thinking late into the night, but by ten he was sleepy and went to bed. The next day he awakened very late, around ten, made his breakfast and ate it before washing or shaving. He felt a little tired. He had not shaved and his hair was uncombed. But after he had eaten, instead of going into the bathroom he wandered from room to room, leafed through a magazine, and finally was delighted to find a light switch that had not been attached, and set to work. Someone knocked: the boy from the café bringing his lunch, as he had arranged the day before. He sat down at his table just as he was, ate without appetite before the food had a chance to cool, and began to smoke, lying on the couch in the downstairs room. When he awakened, annoyed at having fallen asleep, it was four o'clock. He bathed then, shaved carefully, dressed and wrote two letters, one to Lucienne, the other to the three girls. It was already very late, and growing dark. Nonetheless he walked to the village to mail his letters and returned without having met anyone. He went upstairs and out onto the terrace: the sea and the night were conversing on the beach and above the ruins. Mersault reflected. The memory of this wasted day embittered him. Tonight, at least, he would work, do something, read or go out and walk through the night. The garden gate creaked: his dinner was coming. He was hungry, ate happily, then felt unable to leave the house. He decided to read late in bed. But after the first pages his eyes closed, and the next morning he woke up late.

In the days that followed, Mersault tried to struggle against this encroachment. As the days passed, filled by the creak of the gate and countless cigarettes, he was disconcerted by the variance between the gesture which had brought him to this life and this life itself. One evening he wrote Lucienne to come, deciding to break this solitude from which he had expected so much. After the letter was sent, he was filled with a secret shame, but once Lucienne arrived the shame dissolved in a kind of mindless eager joy to rediscover a familiar being and the easy life her presence signified. He made a fuss over her, and Lucienne seemed almost surprised by his solicitude, when she wasn't preoccupied with her carefully pressed white linen dresses.

He took walks now, but with Lucienne. He recovered his complicity with the world, but by resting his hand on Lucienne's shoulder. Taking refuge in humanity, he escaped his secret dread. Within two days, however, Lucienne bored him. And this was the moment she chose to ask him to let her live there. They were at dinner, and Mersault had simply refused, not raising his eyes from his plate.

After a pause, Lucienne had added in a neutral tone of voice: "You don't love me."

Mersault looked up. Her eyes were full of tears. He relented: "But I never said I did, my child."

"I know," Lucienne said, "and that's why."

Mersault stood up and walked to the window. Between the pines, the stars throbbed in the night sky. And never had Patrice felt, along with his dread, so much disgust as at this moment for the days they had just passed together. "You're a lovely girl, Lucienne. I can't see any further than that. It's all I ask of you. It has to be enough for the two of us."

"I know," Lucienne said. She was sitting with her back to Patrice, scoring the tablecloth with the tip of her knife. He walked over to her and rested a hand on the nape of her neck.

"Believe me, there is no such thing as great suffering, great regret, great memory . . . Everything is forgotten, even a great love. That's what's sad about life, and also what's wonderful about it. There is only a way of looking at things, a way that comes to you every once in a while. That's why it's good to have had love in your life after all, to have had an unhappy passion—it gives you an alibi for the vague despairs we all suffer from." After a pause, he added: "I don't know if you understand what I mean."

"I think I understand." She suddenly turned her head toward Mersault. "You're not happy."

"I will be," Mersault said violently. "I have to be. With this night, this sea, and this flesh under my fingers." He had turned back toward the window and tightened his hand over the nape of Lucienne's neck. She said nothing.

Then, without looking at him, "At least you feel friendly toward me, don't you?"

Patrice knelt beside her and gently bit her shoulder. "Friendly, yes, the way I feel friendly toward the night. You are the pleasure of my eyes, and you don't know what a place such joy can have in my heart."

She left the next day. And the day after that Mersault was unable to stand himself, and drove to Algiers. He went first to the House above the World. His friends promised to come to see him at the end of the month. Then he decided to visit his old neighborhood.

His apartment had been rented to a man who ran a café. He inquired after the barrelmaker, but no one knew anything—someone thought he had gone to Paris to look for work. Mersault walked through the streets. At the restaurant, Celeste had aged—but not much; René was still there, with his tuberculosis and his solemn expression. They were all glad to see Patrice again, and he felt moved by this encounter.

"Hey, Mersault," Celeste told him, "you haven't changed. Still the same!"

"Yes," Mersault said. He marveled at the strange blindness by which men, though they are so alert to what changes in themselves, impose on their friends an image chosen for them once and for all. He was being judged by what he had been. Just as dogs don't change character, men are dogs for one another. And precisely to the degree that Celeste, René, and the others had known him, he had become as alien and remote to them as an uninhabited planet. Yet he left them with affectionate farewells. And just outside the restaurant he ran into Marthe. As soon as he saw her he realized that he had almost forgotten her and that at the same time he had wanted to meet her. She still had her painted goddess's face. He desired her vaguely but without conviction. They walked together.

"Oh, Patrice," she said, "I'm so glad! What's become of you?"

"Nothing, as you can see. I'm living in the country."

"Wonderful. I've always dreamed of living in the

country." And after a silence: "You know, I'm not angry at you or anything."

"Yes," Mersault said, laughing, "you've managed to console yourself."

Then Marthe spoke in a tone of voice he did not recognize. "Don't be nasty, Patrice. I knew it would end like this some day. You were a funny guy. And I was nothing but a little girl. That's what you always used to say . . . Of course when it happened I was furious. But finally I told myself, 'He's unhappy.' And you know, it's funny, I don't know how to say it, but that was the first time that what we . . . that what happened between us made me feel sad and happy at the same time."

Surprised, Mersault stared at her. He suddenly realized that Marthe had always been very decent with him. She had accepted him as he was and had spared him a great deal of loneliness. He had been unfair: while his imagination and vanity had given her too much importance, his pride had given her too little. He discovered the cruel paradox by which we always deceive ourselves twice about the people we love—first to their advantage, then to their disadvantage. Today he understood that Marthe had been genuine with him—that she had been what she was, and that he owed her a good deal. It was beginning to rain—just enough to reflect the lights of the street; through the shining drops he saw Marthe's suddenly serious face and felt overcome by a burst of gratitude he could not express—in the old days he might have taken it for a kind of love. But he could find only stiff words: "You know, Marthe, I'm very fond of you. Even now, if there's anything I could do . . ."

She smiled: "No. I'm young still. And I don't do without . . ."

He nodded. What a distance there was between them, and yet what complicity! He left her in front of her own house. She had opened her umbrella, saying, "I hope we'll see each other again."

"Yes," Mersault said. She gave him a sad little smile. "Oh, that's your little girl's face." She had stepped into the doorway and closed her umbrella. Patrice held out his hand and smiled in his turn. "Till next time, image." She hugged him quickly, kissed him on both cheeks, and ran upstairs. Mersault, standing in the rain, still felt Marthe's cold nose and warm lips on his cheeks. And that sudden, disinterested kiss had all the purity of the one given him by the freckled little whore in Vienna.

Then he went to find Lucienne, slept at her apartment, and asked her to walk with him on the boulevards. It was almost noon when they came downstairs. Orange boats were drying in the sun like fruit cut in quarters. The double flock of pigeons and their shadows swooped down to the docks and up again in a long, slow curve. The sun was brilliant and the air grew stifling. Mersault watched the red-and-black steamer slowly gain the channel, put on speed, and gradually veer toward the streak of light glistening where the sky met the sea. For the onlookers, there is a bitter sweetness in every departure. "They're lucky," Lucienne said.

"Yes." He was thinking "No"—or at least that he didn't envy them their luck. For him, too, starting over, departures, a new life had a certain luster, but he knew that only the impotent and the lazy attach happiness to such things. Happiness implied a choice, and within that choice a concerted will, a lucid desire. He could hear Zagreus: "Not the will to renounce, but the will to happiness." He had his arm around Lucienne, and her warm breast rested in his hand.

That same evening, as he drove back to the Chenoua, Mersault felt an enormous silence in himself as he faced the swelling waves and the steep hillsides. By making the gesture of a fresh start, by becoming aware of his past, he had defined what he wanted and what he did not want to be. Those wasted days he had been ashamed of seemed dangerous but necessary now. He might have foundered then and missed his one chance, his one justification. But after all, he had to adapt himself to everything.

Rounding one curve after the next, Mersault steeped himself in this humiliating yet priceless truth: the conditions of the singular happiness he sought were getting up early every morning, taking a regular swim—a conscious hygiene. He drove very fast, resolved to take advantage of his discovery in order to establish himself in a routine which would henceforth require no further effort, to harmonize his own breathing with the deepest rhythm of time, of life itself.

The next morning he got up early and walked down to the sea. The sky was already brilliant, and the morning full of rustling wings and crying birds. But the sun was only touching the horizon's curve, and when Mersault stepped into the still-lusterless water, he seemed to be swimming in an indeterminate darkness until, as the sun climbed higher, he thrust his arms into streaks of icy red and gold. Then he swam back to land and walked up to his house. His body felt alert and ready for whatever the day might bring. Every morning, now, he came downstairs just before sunrise, and this first action controlled the rest of his day. Moreover, these swims exhausted him, but at the same time, because of the fatigue and the energy they afforded, they gave his entire day a flavor of abandonment and joyful lassitude. Yet the hours still seemed long to him—he had not yet detached time from a carcass of habits which still littered the past. He had nothing to do, and his time stretched out, measureless, before him. Each minute recovered its miraculous value, but he did not yet recognize it for what it was. Just as the days of a journey seem interminable whereas in an office the trajectory from Monday occurs in a flash, so Mersault, stripped of all his props, still tried to locate them in a life which had nothing but itself to consider. Sometimes he picked up his watch and stared as the minute hand shifted from one number to the next, marveling that five minutes should seem so interminable. Doubtless that watch opened the way—a painful and tormenting way—which leads to the supreme art of doing nothing. He learned to walk; sometimes in the afternoon he would walk along the beach as far as the ruins of Tipasa; then he would lie down among the wormwood bushes, and with his hands on the warm stone would open his eyes and his heart to the intolerable grandeur of that seething sky. He matched the pounding of his blood with the violent pulsation of the sun at two o'clock, and deep in the fierce fragrance, deafened by the invisible insects, he watched the sky turn from white to deep-blue, then pale to green, pouring down its sweetness upon the still-warm ruins. He would walk home early then, and go to bed. In this passage from sun to sun, his days were organized according to a rhythm whose deliberation and strangeness became as necessary to him as had been his office, his restaurant, and his sleep in his mother's room. In both cases, he was virtually unconscious of it. But now, in his hours of lucidity, he felt that time was his own, that in the brief interval which finds the sea red and leaves it green, something eternal was represented for him in each second. Beyond the curve of the days he glimpsed neither superhuman happiness nor eternity—happiness was human, eternity ordinary. What mattered was to humble himself, to organize his heart to match the rhythm of the days instead of submitting their rhythm to the curve of human hopes.

Just as there is a moment when the artist must stop, when the sculpture must be left as it is, the painting untouched—just as a determination *not to know* serves the maker more than all the resources of clairvoyance—so there must be a minimum of ignorance in order to perfect a life in happiness. Those who lack such a thing must set about acquiring it: unintelligence must be earned.

On Sundays, Mersault played pool with Perez. The old fisherman, one arm a stump cut off above the elbow, played pool in a peculiar fashion, puffing out his chest and leaning his stump on the cue. When they went out fishing in the morning, Perez rowed with the same skill, and Mersault admired the way he would stand in the boat pushing one oar with his chest, the other with his good hand. The two men got along well. After the morning's fishing, Perez cooked cuttlefish in a hot sauce, stewing them in their own ink, and soaking up the black juice left in the pan with pieces of bread. As they sat in the fisherman's kitchen over the sooty stove, Perez never spoke, and Mersault was grateful to him for this gift of silence. Sometimes, after his morning swim, he would see the old man putting his boat in the sea, and he would join him. "Shall I come with you, Perez?"

"Get in."

They put the oars in the locks and rowed together, Mersault being careful not to catch his feet
in the trawling hooks. Then they would fish, and
Mersault would watch the lines, gleaming to the
water's surface, black and wavering underneath.
The sun broke into a thousand fragments on the sea,
and Mersault breathed the heavy stifling smell that
rose from it like fumes. Sometimes Perez pulled in
a little fish he would throw back, saying: "Go home
to your mother." At eleven they rowed home and
Mersault, his hands glistening with scales and his
face swollen with sun, waited in his cool, dark house
while Perez prepared a pan of fish they would eat
together in the evening. Day after day, Mersault
let himself sink into his life as if he were sliding into
water. And just as the swimmer advances by the
complicity of his arms and the water which bears
him up, helps him on, it was enough to make a few
essential gestures—to rest one hand on a tree-
trunk, to take a run on the beach—in order to keep
himself intact and conscious. Thus he became one
with a life in its pure state, he rediscovered a paradise given only to the most private or the most intelligent animals. At the point where the mind denies the mind, he touched his truth and with it his
extreme glory, his extreme love.

Thanks to Bernard, he also mingled with the life
of the village. He had been obliged to send for Bernard to treat some minor indisposition, and since
then they had seen each other repeatedly, with

pleasure. Bernard was a silent man, but he had a kind of bitter wit that cast a gleam in his horn-rimmed glasses. He had practiced medicine a long time in Indochina, and at forty had retired to his corner of Algeria, where for several years he had led a tranquil life with his wife, an almost mute Indochinese who wore Western clothes and arranged her hair in a bun. Bernard's capacity for indulgence enabled him to adapt himself to any milieu. He liked the whole village, and was liked in return. He took Mersault on his rounds. Mersault already knew the owner of the café, a former tenor who would sing behind his bar and between two beats of *Tosca* threaten his wife with a beating. Patrice was asked to serve with Bernard on the holiday committee, and on July 14 they walked through the streets in tricolor armbands or argued with the other committee members sitting around a zinc table sticky with aperitifs as to whether the bandstand should be decorated with ferns or palms. There was even an attempt to lure him into an electoral contest, but Mersault had had time to know the mayor, who had "presided over the destiny of his commune" (as he said) for the last decade, and this semi-permanent position inclined him to regard himself as Napoleon Bonaparte. A wealthy grapegrower, he had had a Greek-style house built for himself, and proudly showed it to Mersault. It consisted of a ground floor and a second floor around a courtyard, but the mayor had spared no expense and installed an elevator, which he insisted that Mersault and Bernard ride in. And Bernard commented placidly: "Very smooth." The visit had inspired Mersault with a profound admiration for the mayor, and he and Bernard wielded all their influence to keep him in the office he deserved on so many counts.

In springtime, the little village with its close-set red roofs between the mountain and the sea overflowed with flowers—roses, hyacinths, bougainvilleas—and hummed with insects. Afternoons, Mersault would walk out onto his terrace and watch the village dozing under the torrent of light. Local history consisted of a rivalry between Morales and Bingues, two rich Spanish landowners whom a series of speculations had transformed into millionaires, in the grip of a terrible rivalry. When one bought a car, he chose the most expensive make; but the other, who would buy the same make, would add silver door handles. Morales was a genius at such tactics. He was known in the village as the King of Spain, for on each occasion he triumphed over Bingues, who lacked imagination. During the war, when Bingues pledged several hundred thousand francs for a national bond drive, Morales had declared: "I'll do better than that, I'll give my son." And he had made his son, who was too young to be mobilized, volunteer. In 1925, Bingues had driven out from Algiers in a magnificent racing Bugatti; two weeks later, Morales had built himself a hangar and bought a plane. The plane was still sleeping in its hangar, and was shown to visitors on Sundays. Bingues called Morales "that barefoot beggar," and Morales referred to Bingues as "that lime kiln."

Bernard took Mersault to visit Morales, who welcomed them warmly to his huge farm, humming with wasps and fragrant with grapes. Wearing espadrilles and shirtsleeves because he could not endure a jacket and shoes, Morales showed them the airplane, the son's medal framed in the living room, and explained the necessity of keeping foreigners out of Algeria (he was naturalized, "but that Bingues, for instance . . ."), then led them to inspect his latest acquisition. They walked through an enormous vineyard in the middle of which was a cleared space where a kind of Louis XV salon had been set up, each piece made of the most precious woods and fabrics. Thus Morales could receive visitors on his grounds. When Mersault courteously asked what happened when it rained, Morales shifted his cigar and without even blinking answered: "I replace it." On his way home, Mersault spent the time arguing with Bernard over the difference between the *nouveau riche* and the poet. Morales, according to Bernard, was a poet. Mersault declared he would have made a splendid Roman emperor during the decline.

Some time later, Lucienne came to the Chenoua for a few days, then left. One Sunday morning, Claire, Rose, and Catherine paid Mersault a visit, as they had promised. But Patrice was already very far from the state of mind that had driven him to Algiers during the first days of his retreat. He was glad to see them again, nevertheless, and brought Bernard to meet them at the stop where the big yellow bus let them off. It was a magnificent day, the village full of the fine red carts of itinerant butchers, flowers everywhere, and the villagers dressed in bright colors. At Catherine's request they took a table at the café, and the girls marveled at all this brilliant life, divining the sea's presence behind the wall they leaned against. As they were leaving, an astonishing burst of music exploded in a nearby street: the toreador song from *Carmen*, but performed with an exuberance that prevented the instruments from keeping in tune or time. "The gymnastic society," Bernard explained. Then some twenty strange musicians appeared, each puffing on a different kind of wind instrument. They marched toward the café, and behind them, his hat worn over a handkerchief on the back of his head, fanning himself with a cheap fan, appeared Morales. He had hired these musicians in the city because, as he explained, "With this depression, life around here is too sad." He sat down at a table and grouped the musicians around him, where they finished their rendition. The café was crowded. Then Morales stood up and announced with tremendous dignity, making a sweeping movement toward the audience: "At my request, the orchestra will play 'Toreador' again."

As they left, the girls were choking with laughter, but once they reached Mersault's house and the cool shade of the rooms, which emphasized the dazzling whiteness of the sun-drenched garden walls, they discovered a silent harmony that Catherine expressed by the desire to take a sunbath on the terrace. Mersault walked Bernard home. This was the second time the doctor had glimpsed something of Mersault's life; they had never confided in each other, Mersault conscious that Bernard was not a happy man, and Bernard rather baffled by Mersault's way of life. They parted without a word. Mersault and the girls decided to make an excursion the following day, starting very early. The Chenoua was high and difficult to climb—ahead of them lay a splendid day of sunlight and fatigue.

At dawn they climbed the first steep slopes. Rose and Claire walked ahead, Patrice and Catherine following. No one spoke. Gradually they rose above the sea, still pale in the morning mist. Patrice felt he belonged to the mountain, with its pelt of saffron blossoms, his eager but weakening body a part of the icy springs, the shadows, and the sunlight. They entered into the concentrated effort of climbing, the morning air sharp in their lungs, determined to conquer the slope. Rose and Claire, exhausted, began to slow down. Catherine and Patrice walked on, and soon lost sight of the other two.

"Are you all right?" Patrice asked.

"Yes, it's beautiful."

The sun rose in the sky, and with it a hum of

insects swelled in the growing warmth. Soon Patrice took off his shirt and walked on bare-chested. Sweat ran down his shoulders where the skin had peeled with sunburn. They took a little path that seemed to follow the mountainside. The grass was wetter here; soon a sound of springs greeted them, and in a hollow they almost stumbled over the sudden gush of coolness and shade. They sprinkled each other, drank a little, and Catherine stretched out on the grass while Patrice, his hair black with water and curling over his forehead, stared blinking over the landscape that was covered with ruins, gleaming roads, and splinters of sunlight. Then he sat down beside Catherine.

"While we're alone, Mersault, tell me—are you happy now?"

"Look," Mersault said. The road trembled in the sun, and the air was filled with a thousand colored specks. He smiled and rubbed his arms.

"Yes, but . . . Well, I wanted to ask you—of course you don't have to answer if you don't want to . . ." She hesitated: "Do you love your wife?"

Mersault smiled: "That's not essential." He gripped Catherine's shoulder and shook his head, sprinkling water into her face. "You make the mistake of thinking you have to choose, that you have to do what you want, that there are conditions for happiness. What matters—all that matters, really— is the will to happiness, a kind of enormous, ever-present consciousness. The rest—women, art, success—is nothing but excuses. A canvas waiting for our embroideries."

"Yes," Catherine said, her eyes filled with sunlight.

"What matters to me is a certain quality of happiness. I can only find it in a certain struggle with its opposite—a stubborn and violent struggle. Am I happy? Catherine! You know the famous formula —'If I had my life to live over again'—well, I would live it over again just the way it has been. Of course you can't know what that means."

"No."

"And I don't know how to tell you. If I'm happy, it's because of my bad conscience. I had to get away and reach this solitude where I could face— in myself, I mean—what had to be faced, what was sun and what was tears . . . Yes, I'm happy, in human terms."

Rose and Claire arrived. They shouldered their knapsacks. The path still followed the mountainside, keeping them in a zone of dense vegetation, prickly pears, olive trees, and jujubes. They passed Arabs on donkeys. Then they climbed again. The sun pounded now on each stone in the path. At noon, crushed by the heat, drunk on fragrance and fatigue, they flung down their knapsacks and gave up reaching the top. The slopes were sheer and full of sharp flints. A wizened oak sheltered them in its circle of shade. They took provisions out of the knapsacks and ate. The whole mountain quivered under the light. The cicadas were deafening as the heat assailed them under their oak. Patrice threw himself on the ground and pressed his chest against the stones, inhaling the scorched aroma. Under his belly he could feel the faint throbs of the mountain that seemed to be in labor. This regular pulse and the unremitting song of the insects between the hot stones finally put him to sleep.

When he awakened he was covered with sweat, and every muscle ached. It must have been three in the afternoon. The girls had vanished, but soon he heard their laughter and shouts. It was cooler now, time to go back down. At this moment, as they were about to start, Mersault fainted for the first time. When he came to, he saw the cobalt sea between three anxious faces. They walked on more slowly. On the last slopes, Mersault asked for a rest. The sea was turning green along with the sky, and the horizon began to blur. On the foothills that stretched from the Chenoua around the little bay, the cypresses blackened slowly. No one spoke, until Claire said: "You look tired."

"I'm not surprised. Are you?"

"It's none of my business, but I don't think this place is good for you. It's too near the sea—too damp. Why don't you go live in France—in the mountains?"

"This place isn't good for me, Claire, but I'm happy here. I feel in harmony with it."

"Well, then you could be in harmony—longer."

"No one is happy relatively—for a longer or

shorter time. You're happy or you're not. That's all. And death has nothing to do with it—death is an accident of happiness, in that case." No one spoke.

After a long pause, Rose said: "I'm not convinced." They returned slowly as night was falling.

Catherine decided to send for Bernard. Mersault was in his room; beyond the shifting shadow of the windowpanes he could see the white patch of the parapet, the sea like a strip of dark linen undulating in the transparent air, and beyond it the night sky, paler but starless. He felt weak, and his weakness made him mysteriously lighter, gayer, and his mind grew more lucid. When Bernard knocked, Mersault sensed he would tell him everything. Not that his secret was a burden; it was not that kind of secret. If he had kept it till now, it was because in certain circles a man keeps his thoughts to himself, knowing they will offend the prejudices and stupidity of others. But today, after his exhaustion, there was a sudden longing in his body to confide. It was the way an artist, after carefully molding and caressing his work, at last feels the need to show it, to communicate with men—Mersault had the feeling he was going to speak now. And without being certain he would do so, he waited impatiently for Bernard.

From downstairs, two bursts of laughter made him smile. And at that moment Bernard came into the room. "Well?"

"Well, here I am," Mersault said. Bernard listened to his chest, but he could tell nothing—he wanted to have an X ray taken, if Mersault could manage to get to Algiers. "Later," Mersault replied.

Bernard said nothing and sat down on the windowsill. "I don't like being sick myself," he said. "I know what it is. Nothing is uglier or more degrading than sickness."

Mersault was unconcerned. He got up from his chair, offered Bernard a cigarette, lit his own, and said with a laugh: "Can I ask you a question, Bernard?"

"Of course."

"You never swim, you're never on the beach— why did you pick this place to live in?"

"Oh, I don't know exactly. It was a long time ago." After a pause he added: "Besides, I've always acted out of rancor. It's better now. Before, I wanted to be happy, to do what had to be done, to settle down somewhere I really wanted to be, for instance. But sentimental anticipation is always wrong. We have to live the way it's easiest for us to live—not forcing ourselves. I suppose it sounds a little cynical, but it's also the point of view you have to take to survive. In Indochina I ran all over the place. Here—here I just ruminate. That's all."

"Yes," Mersault said, still smoking, deep in his armchair and staring at the ceiling. "But I'm not sure that all sentimental anticipation, as you call it, is wrong. Only unreasonable sometimes. In any case, the only experiences that interest me are precisely the ones where everything turns out to be the way you hoped it would."

Bernard smiled. "Yes, a ready-made destiny."

"A man's destiny," Mersault said without moving, "is always passionately interesting, if he achieves it passionately. And for some men, a passionate destiny is always a ready-made destiny."

"Yes," Bernard said. And he stood up deliberately and stared out at the night for a moment, his back to Mersault. He went on without looking at him: "You're the only man besides myself around here who lives alone. I don't mean your wife and your friends downstairs. I know those are episodes. Still, even so, you seem to love life more than I do." He turned around. "Because for me, loving life is not going for a swim. It's living in intoxication, intensity. Women, adventures, other countries . . . It's action, making something happen. A burning, marvelous life. What I mean is—I want you to understand me—" He seemed ashamed of his excitement. "I love life too much to be satisfied with nature." Bernard put away his stethoscope and closed his bag.

Mersault said: "Actually, you're an idealist." And he had the sense that everything was enclosed in that moment which shifts from birth to death, that everything was judged and consecrated then.

"That's because, you see," Bernard said with a kind of sadness, "the opposite of an idealist is too often a man without love."

"Don't believe it," Mersault said, holding out his hand.

Bernard held his hand a long time. "To think the

way you do," he said smiling, "you have to be a man who lives either on a tremendous despair, or on a tremendous hope."

"On both, perhaps."

"Oh, I wasn't asking!"

"I know," Mersault said seriously. But when Bernard was at the door, Mersault, impelled by a sudden need, called him back.

"Yes?" the doctor said, turning around.

"Are you capable of feeling contempt for a man?"

"I think so."

"On what conditions?"

The doctor reflected. "It's quite simple, I think. In cases when he was motivated by expediency or a desire for money."

"That *is* simple," Mersault said. "Goodnight, Bernard."

"Goodnight."

Alone, Mersault reflected. At the point he had now reached, another man's contempt left him indifferent. But he recognized in Bernard profound resonances that brought the two of them together. It seemed intolerable that a part of himself should condemn the rest. Had he acted out of expediency? He had become aware of the essential and immoral truth that money is one of the surest and swiftest means of acquiring one's dignity. He had managed to dispel the bitterness which besets any decent soul aware of the vile iniquities of the birth and growth of a splendid fate. This sordid and revolting curse, whereby the poor end in poverty the life they have begun in poverty, he had rejected by using money as a weapon, opposing hatred with hatred. And out of this beast-to-beast combat, the angel sometimes emerged, intact, wings and halo and all, in the warm breath of the sea. It would be as it had been: he had said nothing to Bernard, and his creation would henceforth remain secret.

The girls left around five o'clock in the afternoon of the next day. As they got into the bus, Catherine turned back: "Goodbye, sea," she said.

A moment later, three laughing faces were staring at Mersault out of the rear window, and the yellow bus vanished like a huge golden insect into the sun. Though clear, the sky was a little heavy. Mersault, standing alone in the road, felt a deep sense of deliverance tinged with melancholy. Only today did his solitude become real, for only today did he feel bound to it. And to have accepted that solitude, to know that henceforth he was the master of all his days to come, filled him with the melancholy that is attached to all greatness.

Instead of taking the highway, he returned through the carob trees and the olives, following a little path that wound around the foothills and came out behind his house. He squashed several olives, and noticed that the path was speckled with these black ovals. At the summer's end, the carobs drench all Algeria with the smell of love, and in the evening or after the rain, it is as if the entire earth were resting, after giving itself to the sun, its womb drenched with a sperm smelling of bitter almonds. All day, their odor had poured down from the huge trees, heavy and oppressive. On this little path at twilight, in the released exhalations of earth, the fragrance grew light, scarcely apparent to Patrice's nostrils—like a mistress you walk with in the street after a long stifling afternoon, and who looks at you, shoulder to shoulder, among the lights and the crowd.

Amid that smell of love and squashed, fragrant fruit, Mersault realized then that the season was ending. A long winter would begin. But he was ready for it, he would wait. From this path he could not see the sea, but he could glimpse on the mountaintop certain reddish mists which heralded the dark. On the ground, patches of sunshine paled among the shadows of the foliage. Mersault sniffed the bitter fragrance which consecrated his wedding to the earth this afternoon. The evening falling on the world, on the path between the olives and the gum trees, on the vines and the red soil, near the sea which whispered softly, this evening flowed into him like a tide. So many evenings had promised him happiness that to experience this one as happiness itself made him realize how far he had come, from hope to conquest. In the innocence of his heart, Mersault accepted this green sky and this love-soaked earth with the same thrill of passion and desire as when he had killed Zagreus in the innocence of his heart.

5

In January, the almond trees bloomed. In March, the pear, peach, and apple trees were covered with blossoms. The next month, the streams gradually swelled, then returned to a normal flow. Early in May, the hay was cut, and the oats and barley at the month's end. Already the apricots were ripening. In June, the early pears appeared with the major crops. The streams began to dry up, and the heat grew more intense. But the earth's blood, shrinking here on the coast, made the cotton bloom farther inland and sweetened the first grapes. A great hot wind arose, parching the land and spreading brushfires everywhere. And then, suddenly, the year changed direction: hurriedly, the grape harvests were brought to an end. The downpours of September and October drenched the land. No sooner was the summer's work done than the first sowing began, while the streams and springs suddenly swelled to torrents with the rain. At the year's end, the wheat was already sprouting in some fields; on others plowing had only just been finished. A little later, the almond trees were once again white against the ice-blue sky. The new year had begun in the earth, in the sky. Tobacco was planted, vines cultivated and fertilized, trees grafted. In the same month, the medlars ripened. Again, the haymaking, the harvesting, the summer plowing. Halfway through the year, the ripe fruits, juicy and sticky, were served on every table: between one threshing and the next, the men ate the figs, peaches, and pears greedily. During the next grape harvest, the sky grew overcast. Out of the north, silent flocks of black starlings and thrushes passed over—for them the olives were already ripe. Soon after they had flown away, the olives were gathered. The wheat sprouted a second time from the viscous soil. Huge clouds, also from the north, passed over the sea, then the land, brushing the water with foam and leaving it smooth and icy under a crystal sky. For several days there were distant, silent flashes in the sky. The first cold spells set in.

During this period, Mersault took to his bed for the first time. Bouts of pleurisy confined him to his room for a month. When he got up, the foothills of the Chenoua were covered with flowering trees, all the way to the sea's edge. Never had spring touched him so deeply. The first night of his convalescence, he walked across the fields for a long time—as far as the hill where the ruins of Tipasa slept. In a silence violated only by the silky sounds of the sky, the night lay like milk upon the world. Mersault walked along the cliff, sharing the night's deep concentration. Below him the sea whispered gently. It was covered with velvety moonlight, smooth and undulating, like the pelt of some animal. At this hour of night, his life seemed so remote to him, he was so solitary and indifferent to everything and to himself

as well, that Mersault felt he had at last attained
what he was seeking, that the peace which filled
him now was born of that patient self-abandonment
he had pursued and achieved with the help of this
warm world so willing to deny him without anger.
He walked lightly, and the sound of his own footsteps seemed alien to him, familiar too, no doubt,
but familiar the way the rustling of animals in the
mastic bushes was familiar, or the breaking waves,
or the rhythm of the night itself in the sky overhead.
And he could feel his own body too, but with the
same external consciousness as the warm breath of
this spring night and the smell of salt and decay that
rose from the beach. His actions in the world, his
thirst for happiness, Zagreus' terrible wound bar-
ing brain and bone, the sweet, uncommitted hours
in the House above the World, his wife, his hopes,
and his gods—all this lay before him, but no more
than one story chosen among so many others without any valid reason, at once alien and secretly familiar, a favorite book which flatters and justifies
the heart at its core, but a book someone else has
written. For the first time, Mersault was aware of
no other reality in himself than that of a passion for
adventure, a desire for power, a warm and an intelligent instinct for a relationship with the world—
without anger, without hatred, without regret. Sitting on a rock he let his fingers explore its crannies
as he watched the sea swell in silence under the
moon. He thought of Lucienne's face he had ca-

ressed, and of the warmth of her lips. The moon poured its long, straying smiles like oil on the water's smooth surface—the sea would be warm as a mouth, and as soft, ready to yield beneath a man's weight. Motionless now, Mersault felt how close happiness is to tears, caught up in that silent exultation which weaves together the hopes and despairs of human life. Conscious yet alienated, devoured by passion yet disinterested, Mersault realized that his life and his fate were completed here and that henceforth all his efforts would be to submit to this happiness and to confront its terrible truth.

Now he must sink into the warm sea, lose himself in order to find himself again, swim in that warm moonlight in order to silence what remained of the past, to bring to birth the deep song of his happiness. He undressed, clambered down a few rocks, and entered the sea. It was as warm as a body, another body that ran down his arms and clung to his legs with an ineffable yet omnipresent embrace. Mersault swam steadily now, feeling the muscles of his back shift with each stroke. Whenever he raised an arm, he cast sheaves of silver drops upon the sea, sowing under this mute and vivid sky the splendid harvest of happiness; then his arm thrust back into the water, and like a vigorous plowshare tilled the waves, dividing them in order to gain a new support, a firmer hope. Behind him, his feet churned the water into seething foam, producing a strangely distinct hissing noise in the night's silence and solitude. Conscious of this cadence, this vigor, an exultation seized Mersault; he swam faster and soon realized he was far from land, alone in the heart of the night, of the world. Suddenly he thought of the depths which lay beneath him and stopped moving. Everything that was below attracted him like an unknown world, the extension of this darkness which restored him to himself, the salty center of a life still unexplored. A temptation flashed through his mind, but he immediately rejected it in the great joy of his body—he swam harder, farther. Gloriously tired, he turned back toward the shore. At that moment he suddenly entered an icy current and was forced to stop swimming, his teeth chattered, his movements lost their harmony. This surprise of the sea left him bewildered; the chill penetrated his limbs and seared him like the love of some god of clear and impassioned exultation whose embrace left him powerless. Laboriously he returned to the beach, where he dressed facing the sky and the sea, shivering and laughing with happiness.

On his way home, he began to feel faint. From the path sloping up toward his house, he could make out the rocky promontory across the bay, the smooth shafts of the columns among the ruins. Then suddenly the landscape tilted and he found himself leaning against a rock, half-supported by a mastic bush, the fragrance of its crushed leaves strong in his nostrils. He dragged himself back to the house. His body, which had just now carried him to the limits of joy, plunged him into a suffering that gripped his bowels, making him close his eyes. He decided tea would help, but he used a dirty pan to boil the water in, and the tea was so greasy it made him retch. He drank it, though, before he went to bed. As he was pulling off his shoes he noticed how pink his nails were, long and curving over the fingertips of his bloodless hands. His nails had never been like that, and they gave his hands a twisted, unhealthy look. His chest felt as though it were caught in a vise. He coughed and spat several times —only phlegm, though the taste of blood lingered on his tongue. In bed, his body was seized by long spasms of shivering. He could feel the chill rising from every extremity of his body, meeting in his shoulders like a confluence of icy streams, while his teeth chattered and the sheets felt as if they had been soaked. The house seemed enormous, the usual noises swelled to infinity, as if they encountered no wall to put an end to their echoes. He heard the sea, the pebbles rolling under the receding wave, the night throbbing behind his windows, the dogs howling on distant farms. He was hot now, threw back the blankets, then cold again, and drew them up. As he wavered between one suffering and another, between somnolence and anxiety, he suddenly realized he was sick, and anguish overwhelmed him at the thought that he might die in this unconsciousness, without being able to see clearly. The village steeple chimed, but he could not keep count of the strokes.

He did not want to die like a sick man. He did not want his sickness to be what it is so often, an attenuation, a transition to death. What he really wanted was the encounter between his life—a life filled with blood and health—and death. He stood, dragged a chair over to the window and sat down in it, huddling in his blankets. Through the thin curtains, in the places where the material did not fall in folds, he saw the stars. He breathed heavily for a long time, and gripped the arms of his chair to control his trembling hands. He would reconquer his lucidity if he could. "It could be done," he was thinking. And he was thinking, too, that the gas was still on in the kitchen. "It could be done," he thought again. Lucidity too was a long patience. Everything could be won, earned, acquired. He struck his fist on the arm of the chair. A man is not born strong, weak, or decisive. He becomes strong, he becomes lucid. Fate is not in man but around him. Then he realized he was crying. A strange weakness, a kind of cowardice born of his sickness gave way to tears, to childishness. His hands were cold, his heart filled with an immense disgust. He thought of his nails, and under his collarbone he pressed tumors that seemed enormous. Outside, all that beauty was spread upon the face of the world. He did not want to abandon his thirst for life, his jealousy of life. He thought of those evenings above Algiers, when the sound of sirens rises in the green sky and men leave their factories. The fragrance of wormwood, the wildflowers among the ruins, and the solitude of the cypresses in the Sahel generated an image of life where beauty and happiness took on an aspect without the need of hope, a countenance in which Patrice found a kind of fugitive eternity. That was what he did not want to leave—he did not want that image to persist without him. Filled with rebellion and pity, he saw Zagreus' face turned toward the window. Then he coughed for a long time. It was hard to breathe. He was smothering under his blankets. He was cold. He was hot. He was burning with a great confusing rage, his fists clenched, his blood throbbing heavily under his skull; eyes blank, he waited for the new spasm that would plunge him back into the blind fever. The chill came, restoring him to a moist, sealed world in which he silenced the animal rebellion, eyes closed, jealous of his thirst and his hunger. But before losing consciousness, he had time to see the night turn pale behind the curtains and to hear, with the dawn and the world's awakening, a kind of tremendous chord of tenderness and hope which without doubt dissolved his fear of death, though at the same time it assured him he would find a reason for dying in what had been his whole reason for living.

When he awakened, the morning had already begun, and all the birds and insects were singing in the warmth of the sun. He remembered Lucienne was coming today. Exhausted, he crawled back to his bed. His mouth tasted of fever, and he could feel the onset of that fragility which makes every effort arduous and other people so irritating in the eyes of the sick. He sent for Bernard, who came at once, quiet and businesslike as always. He listened to Mersault's chest, then took off his glasses and wiped the lenses. "Bad," was all he would say. He gave Mersault two injections. During the second, Mersault fainted, though ordinarily he was not squeamish. When he came to, Bernard was holding his wrist in one hand and his watch in the other, watching the jerky advance of the second hand. "That lasted fifteen minutes," Bernard said. "Your heart's failing. The next time, you might not come out of it."

Mersault closed his eyes. He was exhausted, his lips white and dry, his breathing a hoarse whistle. "Bernard," he said.

"Yes."

"I don't want to die in a coma. I want to see what's happening—do you understand me?"

"Yes," Bernard said, and gave him several ampules. "If you feel weak, break this open and swallow it. It's adrenalin." As he was leaving, Bernard met Lucienne on her way in. "As charming as ever."

"Is Patrice sick?"

"Yes."

"Is it serious?"

"No, he's all right," Bernard said. And just before he was out the door: "One piece of advice, though—try to leave him alone as much as you can."

"Oh," Lucienne said, "then it can't be anything."

All day long, Mersault coughed and choked. Twice he felt the cold, stubborn chill which would draw him into another coma, and twice the adrenalin rescued him from that dark immersion. And all day long his dim eyes stared at the magnificent landscape. Around four, a large red rowboat appeared on the sea, gradually growing larger, glistening with sunlight, brine, and fish scales. Perez, standing, rowed on steadily. Mersault closed his eyes and smiled for the first time since the day before, though he did not unclench his teeth. Lucienne, who had been fussing around the room, vaguely uneasy, threw herself on the bed and kissed him. "Sit down," Mersault said, "you can stay."

"Don't talk, you'll tire yourself out."

Bernard came, gave injections, left. Huge red clouds moved slowly across the sky.

"When I was a child," Mersault said laboriously, leaning back on the pillow, his eyes fixed on the sky, "my mother told me that was the souls of the dead going to paradise. I was amazed they had red souls. Now I know it means a storm is coming. But it's still amazing."

Night was beginning to fall. Images came. Enormous fantastic animals which nodded over desert landscapes. Mersault gently swept them away, despite his fever. He let only Zagreus' face appear, a sign of blood brotherhood. He who had inflicted death was going to die. And then, as for Zagreus, the lucid gaze he cast upon his life was a man's gaze. Until now he had lived. Now he could talk of his life. Of that great ravaging energy which had borne him on, of that fugitive and generating poetry of life, nothing was left now but the transparent truth which is the opposite of poetry. Of all the men he had carried inside himself, as every man does at the beginning of this life, of all those various rootless, mingling beings, he had created his life with consciousness, with courage. That was his whole happiness in living and dying. He realized now that to be afraid of this death he was staring at with animal terror meant to be afraid of life. Fear of dying justified a limitless attachment to what is alive in man. And all those who had not made the gestures necessary to live their lives, all those who feared and exalted impotence—they were afraid of death because of the sanction it gave to a life in which they had not been involved. They had not lived enough, never having lived at all. And death was a kind of gesture, forever withholding water from the traveler vainly seeking to slake his thirst. But for the others, it was the fatal and tender gesture that erases and denies, smiling at gratitude as at rebellion. He spent a day and a night sitting on his bed, his arms on the night table and his head on his arms. He could not breathe lying down. Lu-

cienne sat beside him and watched him without
speaking a word. Sometimes Mersault looked at her.
He realized that after he was gone, the first man
who put his arms around her would make her
soften, submit. She would be offered—her body,
her breasts—as she had been offered to him, and the
world would continue in the warmth of her parted
lips. Sometimes he raised his head and stared out the
window. He had not shaved, his red-rimmed, hollow eyes had lost their dark luster, and his pale,
sunken cheeks under the bluish stubble transformed
him completely.

His gaze came to rest on the panes. He sighed and
turned toward Lucienne. Then he smiled. And in
his face that was collapsing, even vanishing, the
hard, lucid smile wakened a new strength, a cheer-
ful gravity.

"Better?" Lucienne asked in a whisper.

"Yes." Then he returned to darkness between his
arms. At the limit of his strength and his resistance,
he joined Roland Zagreus for the first time, whose
smile had so exasperated him in the beginning. His
short, gasping breath left a moist cloud on the marble of the night table. And in that sickly warmth
rising toward him from the stone, he felt even more
distinctly the icy tips of his fingers and toes. Even
that revealed life, though, and in this journey from
cold to warm, he discovered the exultation which
had seized Zagreus, thanking life "for allowing him
to go on burning." He was overcome by a violent

and fraternal love for this man from whom he had felt so distant, and he realized that by killing him he had consummated a union which bound them together forever. That heavy approach of tears, a mingled taste of life and death, was shared by them both, he realized now. And in Zagreus' very immobility confronting death he encountered the secret image of his own life. Fever helped him here, and with it an exultant certainty of sustaining consciousness to the end, of dying with his eyes open. Zagreus too had had his eyes open that day, and tears had fallen from them. But that was the last weakness of a man who had not had his share of life. Patrice was not afraid of such weakness. In the pounding of his feverish blood, though it failed to reach the limits of his body, he understood that such weakness would not be his. For he had played his part, fashioned his role, perfected man's one duty, which is only to be happy. Not for long, no doubt. He had destroyed the obstacle, and this inner brother he had engendered in himself—what did it matter if he existed for two or for twenty years? Happiness was the fact that he had existed.

The blanket slipped from Mersault's shoulders, and when Lucienne stood up to cover him, he shuddered at her touch. Since the day he had sneezed in the little square near Zagreus' villa to this moment, his body had served him faithfully, had opened him to the world. But at the same time, it lived a life of its own, detached from the man it represented. For these few years it had passed through a slow decomposition; now it had completed its trajectory, and was ready to leave Mersault, to restore him to the world. In that sudden shudder of which Mersault was conscious, his body indicated once more a complicity which had already won so many joys for them both. Solely for this reason, Mersault took pleasure in that shudder. Conscious, he must be conscious, he must be conscious without deception, without cowardice—alone, face to face—at grips with his body—eyes open upon death. It was a man's business. Not love, not a landscape, nothing but an infinite waste of solitude and happiness in which Mersault was playing his last cards. He felt his breathing weaken. He gasped for air, and in that movement his ruined lungs wheezed. His wrists were cold now, and there was no feeling in his hands at all. Day was breaking.

The new day was cool, filled with the sound of birds. The sun rose quickly, and in a single leap was above the horizon. The earth was covered with gold, with warmth. In the morning, sky and sea were spattered with dancing patches of blue and yellow light. A light breeze had risen, and through the window a breath of salt air cooled Mersault's hands. At noon the wind dropped, the day split open like ripe fruit and trickled down the face of the world, a warm and choking juice in a sudden concert of cicadas. The sea was covered with this golden juice, a sheet of oil upon the water, and gave back to the sun-crushed earth a warm, softening breath which released odors of wormwood, rosemary, and hot stone. From his bed, Mersault received that impact, that offering, and he opened his eyes on the huge, curved, glistening sea irradiated with the smiles of his gods. Suddenly he realized he was sitting on his bed, and that Lucienne's face was very close to his. Slowly, as though it came from his stomach, there rose inside him a stone which approached his throat. He breathed faster and faster, higher and higher. He looked at Lucienne. He smiled without wincing, and this smile too came from inside himself. He threw himself back on the bed, and felt the slow ascent within him. He looked at Lucienne's swollen lips and, behind her, the smile of the earth. He looked at them with the same eyes, the same desire.

"In a minute, in a second," he thought. The ascent stopped. And stone among the stones, he returned in the joy of his heart to the truth of the motionless worlds.

Afterword

A Happy Death draws on memories of Belcourt, the work-ingmen's district where Camus spent his childhood, as well as of his job at the maritime commission, his travels in central Europe in the summer of 1936, in Italy in 1936 and 1937, his sanatorium experiences, and his life in the Fichu house, or the "House above the World," where he lived in November 1936. One reads also episodes in his love life —his two years of marriage with Simone Hié and the break with her, after a stormy scene in Salzburg. Another female figure, difficult to identify, plays an important role in the book. Several more specific questions remain that biographical research may someday answer: Who was Lucienne? Roland Zagreus? Doctor Bernard? etc. For the time being, it seems more useful to sketch a literary genesis than to establish a point-by-point correspondence between a novel and a life.

The first specific mention, in the *Notebooks*, of what was to become *A Happy Death* is a plan of "Part II" that could only have come after the trip to central Europe. The last sketches for the novel date from 1938. The name Mersault occurs as late as January 1939, but by then Camus was concerned with *The Stranger*. Thus *A Happy Death* was conceived and composed between 1936 and 1938. It is contemporary with the first version of *L'Envers et l'endroit* and the final one of *Noces*, and follows the first draft of *Caligula*.

To understand the composition of the novel, it is best to consider the final version first. *A Happy Death* is divided into two parts, each consisting of five chapters: "Natural Death," then "Conscious Death." But the first part consists of only 49 typed pages, scarcely more than a third of the entire 140.

The core of "Natural Death" is the murder of Roland

Zagreus. Mersault, the hero, kills him in the first chapter, takes his money, and falls ill on his return home. The subsequent chapters are flashbacks: to Mersault's ordinary life (Chapter 2), his relations with Marthe and his sexual jealousy (Chapter 3), his long conversation with Zagreus (Chapter 4), and finally the encounter with the barrelmaker Cardona, whose pathetic story is told in Chapter 5. To summarize: an ordinary office worker, Patrice Mersault, the neighbor of a barrelmaker whose life is even more wretched than his own and the lover of a girl whose first lover was the invalid Roland Zagreus, makes the latter's acquaintance through this girl, learns from a conversation with him how he made his fortune, and taking advantage of this confidence, murders him; he then leaves the country, his health uncertain but his wallet full.

The five chapters of "Conscious Death" present Mersault's stay in Prague (Chapter 1), the rest of his journey and his return, through Genoa, to Algiers (Chapter 2), his life in the House above the World (Chapter 3), his departure for the Chenoua, where he moves into a house overlooking the sea (Chapter 4), and finally his pleurisy and death (Chapter 5). To summarize: in Prague, Mersault feels happiness escaping him; he regains his sense of it as he returns to the sun. Back in Algiers, he makes two experiments in happiness: first, by living with three girls in the House above the World; then in an ascetic solitude in the Chenoua, mitigated by visits from his wife Lucienne or from the three friends. He has conquered happiness, and retains it in death itself, evoking Zagreus.

This resumé of the novel suggests its chief theme: how to die a happy man? In other words, how to live as one so that death itself is happy? The first part of the novel is the "wrong side"—*l'envers*—of this problem of a happy life and death, for the hero lacks money, time, and emotional mastery; the second part of the novel, endowing him with financial independence, an organization of time, and peace of heart, is the "right side"—*l'endroit*. This, in summary, is the content and meaning of *A Happy Death* in its final version.

The division into two parts was a belated one. All the sketches for the book's composition until 1938 indicate three parts, and the revisions concern only the arrangement of the chapters. Thus it is not surprising to encounter the dissymmetry (49 pages against 91) which appears in the final plan. The three-part division, as one sketch called "rearrangement" testifies, was more balanced: each part would have had approximately the same number of pages.

The final version indicates a strong contrast, which does not occur in the earlier sketches. Yet contrast, alternation, seems from the start to be the aesthetic motif of the novel, as of Camus's philosophy. In a note proposing to tell "six stories":

story of the brilliant game. Luxury.
story of the workingmen's neighborhood. Death of the mother.
story of the House above the World.
story of sexual jealousy.
story of the man condemned to death.
story of the pursuit of the sun

Camus reveals, by the very order of his list, this concern with alternation. The six stories can be paired. Until August 1937, however, he tried to match the contrast of polarity with a contrast of tenses: certain chapters are written in the present, others in the past. He even tried, in a detailed plan of "Part I," to relate the tenses according to a rigorous system, but later abandoned this formalism, which was not sustained by an internal necessity. Yet a vestige of it persists in the French text as published: the chapter devoted to the House above the World, an evocation of a pure and continuous happiness, is written in the present, as in the initial sketch.

These six stories form the raw material of what was gradually to become a novel. We can retrace the novel's genesis from them—from their metamorphosis and their arrangement.

The first sketches stress the story of the House above the World, which occupies, with that of jealousy, "Part II." Here is the first plan in the *Notebooks:*

Part II:
A. present tense
B. past tense
Chapter A1 The House above the World. Description.
Chapter B1 Recollections. Liaison with Lucienne.
Chapter A2 House above the World. His youth.
Chapter B2 Lucienne describes her infidelities.
Chapter A3 House above the World. Invitation.
Chapter B4 Sexual jealousy. Salzburg. Prague.
Chapter A4 House above the World. Sun.
Chapter B5 Getaway (letter). Algiers. Catches cold, falls sick.
Chapter A5 Starry night. Catherine.

Thus the first part is devoted, as can be seen by a plan sketched after August 1937, to the brilliant game–workingmen's neighborhod pairing: what the "brilliant game" is will be shown, later on, by *The Myth of Sisyphus* in the trinity Don Juanism, pretense, conquest; this game is contrasted with the vicissitudes of life in the "workingmen's neighborhood." Then appears a double antagonism indicated by a sketch dated August 1937:

Part I. His life hitherto.
Part II. Flight.
Part III. Abandonment of compromises and truth in nature.

"Life hitherto" signifies poverty, eight hours of work a day, banality of social relations—in other words, a false mode of being. "The game," about which the *Notebooks* are extremely laconic, must designate a kind of dandyism, an advance on an impoverished life, a delight in personal pleasure, but still false. This antagonism, in the final version of *A Happy Death*, loses its importance, diluted in dialogues and summarized in Mersault's advancement. On the other hand, the conquest of authenticity, by an impulse of flight into solitude and nature, appears in the first sketches and remains the novel's end in every sense.

But *A Happy Death* does not appear to end, in the first sketches, with the hero's death: "craving for death and the sun" we read in one outline; this is only a craving. In another, death is confronted (?), but located at the end of the first part: "Last chapter: pursuit of the sun and death (suicide–natural death)." One notable feature: death and the sun are related. Once a sun, a sensuous image, is replaced by happiness, a moral myth, a decisive step will have been taken toward the final conception. We can date this step August 1937 with the note: "Novel: the man who has realized that in order to live he must be rich, who gives himself up to this conquest of money, succeeds, lives and dies a happy man." For the first time, in the *Notebooks,* we encounter a virtual summary of *A Happy Death,* and it is here that we first find the word "novel."

The main thread of this novel is henceforth clear: it will be an inverted illustration of the proverb: Money does not make happiness. Happiness, through money, becomes the chief theme, as clearly appears at the beginning of the note of November 17, 1937:

Will to happiness.
Part III. Achievement of happiness.

But at this moment the character of Zagreus, who is as
yet only the "invalid," supervenes, in order to enlighten
Mersault as to the problem of the relationships between
money and time and to show him the truth of another
proverbial statement—Time is money, equally true, in the
reverse: Money is time—which will form a fundamental
principle in his art of living, as is testified in the last paragraph of the November 17 note:

> "For a man who is 'well born,' to be happy is to par-
> take of the common lot not with the will to renunciation,
> but with the will to happiness. In order to be happy, time
> is necessary—a great deal of time. Happiness too is a long
> patience. And time is the need for money which robs us
> of it. Time can be bought. Everything can be bought. To
> be rich is to have time to be happy when one is worthy
> of being so."

Thus the various materials of the novel are regrouped
according to the pairing time lost and time won. Time lost
is that of poverty, work, everyday life: the chapter devoted to Mersault's life is entitled "Killing Time," a title
which would also suit the affair with Marthe and the trip
in central Europe; the murder of Zagreus will end this
wretched odyssey of time lost. Time won will be the time
spent in the House above the World and in flight into nature. At this point, on a manuscript page, appears an outline in three parts whose initial chapter, each time, is
devoted to time. The first part consists of seven chapters,
from "Killing Time," which include Mersault's life from
the Algerian adventures to the return from Prague (*i.e.*,
pages 1–75 of the final version): "First from 'killing time,'"
Camus writes, "to 'he felt he was made for happiness.'"

This last phrase occurs in virtually the same form on page 75 of the final version: "he understood at last that he was made for happiness."

The first chapter of the second part is then entitled "Gaining Time"—it concerns the House above the World —and the first chapter of the third part, "Time." If we think of Proust, we see the novel proceeding from time lost, that of work, to time gained or won, that of idleness in the "budding grove" of the House above the World, to time regained, which is harmony with nature in solitude and death, summarized by a succinct note on the manuscript of the last page: "Time." "First does a lot of things and then abandons everything. Does nothing at all. Follows time and above all the seasons (diary!)." Time, having become the standard of happiness, the principal theme, gives the novel its frame and its rhythm. The present/past alternation of the first sketches was not inductive. Now, from the pulverized time of the first part to the atemporal process of the third, the current is to pass through and connect the atonal descriptions to the lyrical accents.

Thus we come to the novel's final form, its contraction into two parts, which can be explained by two reasons: first, Camus's embarrassment regarding the erotic or emotional episodes. He had to restrict them. In the outline mentioned above, the second part, after "Gaining Time," announced "Encounter with Lucienne," then "Catherine's departure." Camus either could not or would not organize enough material under these headings. Subsequently the Zagreus episode became important enough to form the core of a system. The flight into central Europe, which was originally linked to sexual jealousy, was transferred to this system.

But Camus clung to his three-part division. Whence still another outline, the last before the final contraction:

Part I. 1: The workingmen's neighborhood; 2: Patrice Mersault; 3: Patrice and Marthe; 4: (erased) P. and his friends (?); 5: Patrice and Zagreus.

Part II. 1: Murder of Zagreus; 2: flight into anxiety; 3: return to happiness.

Part III. 1: The women and the sun; 2: secret and ardent happiness at Tipasa; 3: the happy death.

The definitive title has been found, but applied to the last chapter. The Zagreus episode has not yet found its proper place. It remains to transfer the murder first to the end and then to the beginning of the first part. Then the second part, reduced to the journey and the return, is too thin—it is integrated into the last part, and a common title, "Conscious Death," sanctions the fusion, evoking a parallel title: "Natural Death." On the other hand, the chapters that were given titles—"The House above the World," then "The Women and the Sun"—now follow without them, in the unusual use of the present indicative following the return from Prague. Thus was rewritten ("rewrite Novel," Camus enjoined himself in June 1938), completed, or at least reworked, *A Happy Death*.

Why wasn't it published? We shall hold to only the purely literary reasons here. According to M. Castex's study of *The Stranger*, the latter supplanted *A Happy Death* in Camus's intentions, and we can see, during August 1937—the critical period of that novel's gestation—the surreptitious appearance of the theme of *The Stranger*. M. Castex quotes this text:

A man who has looked for life where it is ordinarily found (marriage, job, etc.) and who suddenly realizes, reading a fashion magazine, how alien he has been to life (life as it is considered in fashion magazines) . . .

which gives the first formulation of the theme, although it refers to *A Happy Death*.

This hypothesis is correct. We may confirm it by examining the novelistic value of *A Happy Death*. Apparently Camus felt, as he was creating it, the latent defect of his first novel and another fictional possibility.

A work "both clumsily composed and remarkably written," Roger Quilliot notes. It cannot be better put. The stylistic virtues are astonishing, but not those of a novelist. Camus vainly tries to organize and unify his disparate materials. What relation is there between the fictional murder of Zagreus and the chronicle of the actual trip to Prague? between the portrait of the wretched Cardona and the evocation of the House above the World? The disparity in tone aggravates that of the episodes, without our being able to excuse it by a deliberate recourse to contrast: the pathetic, the playful, the vulgar, the curtly descriptive, the warmly sensual, the sun-drenched lyrical alternate without any accommodation to one another. The episodes are too numerous and on occasion overlap. Thus, after Mersault's mother's death, we are made to suffer that of Cardona's mother. The women's parts, especially, are badly handled: the trio of "grinds" is unbalanced by Catherine, who originally—according to the first sketches—had an affair with Mersault, but Lucienne could have availed herself of the same advantage. The outlines call for an affair sometimes with one, sometimes with the other. We also encounter the name of a certain Lucile. Marthe, as seen from a correction, will replace her and assume a part of the roles of both Lucienne and Catherine. She will be the link of time lost, Catherine that of time regained. Certainly Camus is not comfortable with his women! They obstruct the nymphosis of his novel and afford a literary illustration of the proverb: "Grasp all, lose all." In the final version, we feel Camus's effort to establish their respective attributes, to follow their wake or to prepare their entrance. The result is mediocre.

Had he worked still harder, might he have succeeded better? *A Happy Death*, as a novel, is doomed in its principle. "The quality of a novel," as M. Coulet has recently remarked on the genre, "depends on the tension in which are united exact observation and the correction or investigation of the real by the imaginary." No novel escapes this rule. But in *A Happy Death* the elements of observation, *i.e.*, the fragments of autobiography, remain disjointed: memories of the workingmen's neighborhood, of the sanatorium, of the House above the World, of the trip to central Europe, of the female figures are not, in the chemical sense, treated in order to unite in "a whole, a closed and unified world" like Proust's, which *The Rebel* exemplifies. They would form a whole only if reworked by the creative imagination. And the creative imagination, in *A Happy Death*, functions only on the level of style. The invention of episodes or characters is impoverished indeed: neither the murder of Zagreus, inspired by *Man's Fate* or *Crime and Punishment*, nor the character himself attains fictional authenticity. In this impossible novel, only the autobiographical scenes are valid, which are analogous to the vein of "L'Envers et l'Endroit" ("The Wrong Side and The Right Side") and not formally distinct from "L'Ironie" ("Irony") or "La Mort dans l'âme" ("Death in the Soul") or the lyrical evocations related to those of *Noces* (*Nuptials*). The best elements in the novel are not novelistic.

Did Camus feel this so clearly? He never says as much. But it is more than likely that his artistic subconscious at least warned him of the danger and attracted him, without his realizing it, in a more profitable direction. To borrow from Gide a suggestive comparison from the naturalist's domain, within the chrysalis of *A Happy Death* was forming the larva of *The Stranger. A Happy Death* accomplished its deceptive nymphosis, its author took pains to rewrite it, to rework all its parts, but *The Stranger,* like a kind of inspired parasite, derived all the benefit of this labor, which, ultimately, instead of a false novel, was to produce a true *récit.*

We may conclude by a brief parallel between *A Happy Death* and *The Stranger.* (In any exhaustive study, the parallel with *Caligula* would be inescapable.) Roger Quillit has shown that "Mersault is . . . the younger brother of Mersault"; he has pointed out that certain episodes and secondary characters are common to both texts, but he is particularly sensitive to the differences, and can write: "The two plots have no relation . . . ," or: "*A Happy Death* is in no way the matrix of *The Stranger:* it is an altogether different book . . ."

However, despite the obvious differences in plot, structure, and intention, we may see in *A Happy Death* a prefiguration of *The Stranger* and even, setting aside the biological sense of the term, its matrix. To be convinced of this, we need merely compare the structure of the two works: *A Happy Death* in its final version is reduced to two parts. The transition from ternary to binary division signifies for Camus the abandonment of a classical articulation, in which the synthesis of contraries is effected, for the sake of a more personal dialectic in which the contraries are short-circuited. From this point of view, *The Stranger* is merely a tracing of *A Happy Death:* it is also in two parts, and has virtually the same number of chapters (6 and 5 instead of 5 and 5). The scheme of the first part, in both books, is noticeably the same: scenes of everyday life, then conversation with the man with the dog (Salamano or Cardona), then a murder (of Zagreus, moved to

the beginning, by artifice, *in extremis,* or of the Arab).
This murder transfers the hero from the realm of the
factitious to that of truth. Apparently the respective second parts have nothing in common. Certainly the trip to
Prague or the House above the World, elements unas-
similable to a symbolic *récit,* have vanished from *The
Stranger.* But if we consider Mersault in his isolation in the
Chenoua and Meursault in his Algerian prison, we shall
discover, in the rhythm of the visits which distract them,
of the seasons which stir them, of the imponderable time
which conducts them to their final hour, a correspondence.
And if their fate seems quite dissimilar because one has
committed a perfect crime from which he benefits while
the other, a clumsy murderer, becomes the victim of his
judges, we must not forget that their shared problem is that
of the happy death—"The Stranger or a Happy Man" is
is the subtitle of one manuscript—and that both men solve
it victoriously, in harmony with the world and released
from humanity.

This is merely the sketch of a comparison which a close
study, attached less to the substance than to the style of
these two works, could establish in depth. The superiority
of *The Stranger* would be merely emphasized. But may we
not merely say, finally, that *A Happy Death,* not published
by Camus, is a document rather than a work, and that it is
enough in the long run that there figure in this document,
to be accounted for in the dossier of his genius, certain
positive elements? We leave the reader the pleasure of discovering them for himself.

The files in the possession of Mme Camus contain two
versions of *A Happy Death* typed by Camus. The first is
amplified by manuscript additions and corrections that are
typed in the second, along with several variants. In May

and June of 1961, Mme Camus had three copies of a new typescript prepared, representing the first typescript on which the variants of the second are registered in ink. The present edition reproduces this typescript, following the correction of certain errors of transcription. The variants of the second typescript, though not in Camus's hand, were doubtless made with his consent and have been, for the most part, retained.

In this typescript the divisions into chapters are indicated by a blank. We have nonetheless restored the numerals which existed in the first typescript, and which are to be found, as well, in *The Stranger*.

There also exist preparatory dossiers and notes for *A Happy Death,* to which must be added the fragments in the *Notebooks*. These, in manuscript form, but generally in very disjunct fragments, constitute nearly the entire novel, for which there exists no manuscript version except for the third chapter of the second part.

In order to show how the various fragments of the novel have been assembled, a choice of the variants has been made. Those taken from the preparatory dossiers and notes are designated by Ms., those taken from the first typescript by T. When the *Notebooks* have been drawn on, the fact has been indicated. In the case of some chapters, we have been able to compare several manuscript texts, which have been carefully distinguished.

Words or phrases scratched out on the typescript or the manuscript have been put in parentheses in the Notes. Words and phrases in italics indicate variant readings.

The establishment of these notes and variants, as of the text itself, owes a great deal to Mme Camus, whom we herewith thank.

Jean Sarocchi

Notes and
Variants

Part One

Natural
Death

The significance of this title relates to "The Wind at Djemila" in *Noces* (*Nuptials*) and to a manuscript fragment of "Entre oui et non" ("Between Yes and No").

Chapter 1

A series of manuscript pages gives successively chapters 4 and 1. As we know, Chapter 1 was originally Chapter 5.

page 3, line 1
The name Mersault may be regarded as a combination of *mer* (sea) and *soleil* (sun).

page 3, line 2
What is the source of the name Zagreus? Was Camus thinking of Orphism's Dionysos-Zagreus, victim of the Titans, whose heart gave birth to the Theban Dionysos of popular legend? In which case Zagreus would be a Promethean figure, belonging to the type of sacrificial being who affords liberation. This is merely a conjecture.

page 3, line 4
Ms.: deserted. *This was two days after his conversation with Roland.*

page 3, line 8
Ms.: hillside, *like the proud laughter of the golden earth.*

page 3, line 21
Ms.: his gloves. *Everything depended on knowing if the chest was unlocked and the revolver loaded.*

page 3, line 24
knocked. ("You can come in, Mersault," Zagreus said.)

page 3, line 25
Ms.: Zagreus was there in his study by the fire.
T.: Zagreus was there in his study of course, sitting in an
armchair with a blanket over the stumps of his legs.

page 4, line 7
Ms.: rejoiced, *showing all its blue and gleaming teeth,*

page 4, line 8
Ms.: A great icy joy, a *classical dance of the world over
the little valley*

page 6, line 19
Ms.: an expression *that combined the child and the
mandarin. It was the very aspect of truth which smiled at
Mersault out of the sky.*

page 7, line 19
The manuscript text includes another paragraph, beginning "That evening, still in bed, he sent for the neighborhood doctor," which is now to be found at the end of
Chapter 5.

Chapter 2

This is the most laboriously and the least skillfully composed chapter in the novel. It consists of several fragments,
all intended to create the impression of a prosaic and
routine existence. In all the sketches and outlines for *The
Right Death* where it figures, it is located in Part One. In
the *Notebooks* for August 1937, we read: "Part One. His
life hitherto." Or: "Part One. A1. M. Mersault's day seen
from outside. B1. Workingmen's neighborhod of Paris
(*word illegible*). Horse butcher's. Patrice and his family.
The mute. The grandmother." Some of these elements
will be transferred to Chapter 5.

Considerably later an outline specifies: "Part One: 1 the
workingmen's neighborhood; 2 Patrice Mersault . . ." and

at about the same date, two plans for Part One are given as follows on the same page:

Part One.
Mersault goes home. Detail . . . Sunday. His dead mother (the butcher shop across the street *To Man's Noblest Conquest*). Sign: to rent. (His office. His neighbor the barrelmaker. Knock at the door. The barrelmaker asking him to come with him to the graveyard.)
The filthy street.
1 Marthe waits for him impatiently (her jealousies)
. 2 Marthe and her infidelities; jealousy; her first lover Zagreus
3 Zagreus and conversation.

This outline is crossed out and replaced by the following one:

a) Mersault goes home. Detail. Sunday.
b) His house. Horse butcher's. His neighbor the barrelmaker and his sister. (Today M.'s mother died. Story of the . . . *word illegible*)
   At the restaurant: M. Lopez who eats at his table . . . *several words illegible*
c) Marthe
d) Zagreus.

We may note that if the chapter's place is ascertained—it is still the first—its substance as well as its composition is indeterminate; for example, the restaurant scene, initially to come after the description of Mersault's house and Sunday, will be moved to an earlier place in the final version. The barrelmaker's story will be isolated and transferred to Chapter 5.

No complete manuscript exists of this chapter, composed of various fragments, some of which are taken from the first version of "Voix du quartier pauvre" in *L'Envers et l'Endroit* ("The Wrong Side and the Right Side" in *Lyrical and Critical Essays*)

A. *The harbor, the injured man, racing for the truck with Emmanuel.* This part of the text was added much later to the chapter, and in the manuscript ends with "When they reached Belcourt, Mersault got off. Emmanuel went on . . ." Sketches for this text are to be found in the *Notebooks*, I, pp. 23–4.

B. *For the rest of the chapter*, after the arrival at Belcourt, a series of manuscript pages forms an arrangement.

a) *Up to the restaurant.* Mersault's actions are the subject of a fragment which has been added to the typescript. On the manuscript pages, Emmanuel is named Marcel.

page 10, line 17
Ms.: young and vigorous, *under the anonymous jacket*

page 10, line 18
Ms.: joy, *discovery*

page 10, line 21
Ms.: from sports. *And if this knowledge overemphasized the "handsome fellow" aspect in Mersault, at the same time his body inspired an instructive self-confidence.*

b) *Celeste's anecdote.*
This is left blank on the manuscript pages, which merely note, as a transition, the following episode:
"Good for him," Mersault said, in order to say something.
"Oh you can't be a bastard in life. All the same . . ."
This anecdote exists in three manuscript versions, one inserted in the hospital conversations. It was not, therefore, in a café that it was taken from life.

page 10, line 30
The earliest manuscript version contains this sentence:
"Something in this man expressed the intelligence and
frankness inseparable from a simple heart."

page 11, line 15
Ms.: Fine with me.' " *Louis fiddled with the tassels of a
rep cushion . . .*

The name Louis, which preceded that of Mersault, des-
ignates Camus in the hospital fragments.

page 11, line 30
Ms.: the wind was blowing. *He laughed self-indulgently.
But just when Louis stood up to leave, he suddenly said to
him: "You always have to look at life from the right side,
and walk straight ahead." Louis was already out in the
street. He walked very fast, avoided a shoeshine boy,
pushed another away, then stopped short and yielded his
foot to a third.*

  c) *Emmanuel's anecdote.*

  This is sketched in the manuscript pages. It is obviously another anecdote taken from life, but it does
  not exist *in extenso* in manuscript. Another hospital
  recollection? In any case, Emmanuel is too young to
  have participated in the battle of the Marne.

  d) *the owner and his son.*

  e) *the anecdote about Jean Perez,* left blank in the
  manuscript pages. It is taken from the pages of the
  text "l'Hôpital du quartier pauvre."

  f) *Mersault's reflections,* his return home (up to "he
  had kept the best room for himself").

page 12, line 1
Ms.: ate his *banana*

page 12, line 19
Ms.: on his back. *His arms did the rest.*

  g) *the mother's death; the burial.*

Blank on the manuscript pages. This text, developed in the first chapter of *The Stranger*, reveals one of Camus's obsessions: death of the mother, the wife, or even of the mistress. Camus is never tired of writing on this theme.

In what appears to be the earliest text from which this one proceeds, the bereaved is not Mersault (Camus), but a trucker—"inhabitant of the workingmen's neighborhood"—who loses his wife. The text *in extenso* follows:

A young man must have a powerful imagination to believe he can grow old. And were it not for death, few would ever believe they had. Thus this man's life had been surprised by old age. His family's existence had been confined to this neighborhood, where they lived according to the opinion of their neighbors and the pity of the world.

A beautiful woman enjoys—and expects to enjoy —a life of diversion, a life of pleasure. This man's wife had been beautiful, and she had expected to enjoy a life of diversion and pleasure. He was a trucker, and worked hard all during their married life. They had had two daughters, both of whom were married. And a lame son who was a leatherworker and lived with his parents.

At about forty, this woman had been stricken by a terrible disease. She was, etc., enriched by her heedless life. For a decade she dragged out an unendurable existence. This martyrdom lasted so long that those around her . . . she could die.

She had a tubercular nephew who occasionally came to see her. She enjoyed his visits because she felt on an equal footing with him. But he was very young, and his natural cowardice shrank from these (*illegible*) which sapped all his resistance.

One day she died. She was fifty-six. She had married very young. Then her husband realized how old he was. He had worked too hard to notice up till now. People felt sorry for him. In the neighborhood, they looked forward to the funeral. They recalled the husband's deep feeling for the dead woman. The daughters were warned not to cry, so that their father would not give way to his grief. He was urged not to mourn, to take care of himself. Meanwhile, the man dressed in his best clothes. And with his hat in his hand, he watched the arrangements, etc., that was all.

However, he immediately sold his truck, despite his lack of means, paid his debts, and then found himself poor and penniless. He lived with one of his daughters now, spending long days on the balcony. He had left his old neighborhood. On the house where he had lived was a sign: For Rent, and speculation over its meaning never ceased.

Another manuscript, virtually without erasures and obviously subsequent to the one just quoted, gives virtually the same text, but begins with this sentence added to the preceding manuscript, a sentence Camus appears to have valued for its own sake: "A beautiful woman, she had enjoyed—and expected to enjoy—a life of diversion, a life of pleasure." Then: "Her husband was a trucker . . . ," etc. Another modification in the last sentence may be noted: "this sign: For Rent, which always means more than it says."

h) *Mersault's attachment to his room.*

The manuscript pages, after the blank left for the insertion of the mother's death and burial, continue:

But he had had to abandon his studies and his ambitions and take a job. At first he had resisted, he had wanted to live for himself, work, write, have a life of his own. Later on, he had given it all up and tried to expunge his own life. He wakened, etc. (Mersault at the office).

i) *Mersault at the office.*
This text is given *in extenso* in the manuscript pages.
j) *Mersault at home.*
Idem.

page 17, line 19
Ms.: M. Langlois. *M. Langlois had read Courteline.*

page 18, line 1
Ms.: in front of his name *or in an influential position.*

page 18, line 4
Ms.: strutting *and slobbering*

page 18, line 7
Ms.: vegetables. *The secretaries were giggling openly. The old lady bending* (illegible) *glancing up and still writing finally announced: "I should appreciate it, M. Langlois, if you would do without my approval."*

"One to zero," P. *said calmly. And he listened to the thousand noises of the harbor behind the walls* (illegible) *tasting of salt and blood, so remote and yet so close to him.* Then comes the line: *In the evening he returned at 6 o'clock—It was Saturday.*

page 18, line 27
Ms.: pasted *carefully* into a booklet *printed for the purpose*

page 18, line 30
Ms.: beautiful, *sultry*

page 19, line 8
Ms.: silk dress *and cloche hat,*

page 21, line 18
T.: The chapter ends as follows:

> bread. *He scratched his head and walked toward the mirror, meeting himself. He yawned and turned toward his bed. Already he was taking off his shoes. He said: "Another Sunday shot."*

page 21, line 23
Ms. his windows. *He went to bed and slept till the next morning, when he left for his office.* For several years he lived this way, except for certain evenings when Marthe came or when he went out with her, *certain rarer Sundays which he shared with Zagreus and Marthe's girlfriends.*
Here the manuscript pages end.

Chapter 3

Devoted to relations between Marthe and Mersault, this chapter, in the first outlines, was to take its place in the second part of the novel, and was to be subdivided. Thus, in the first outline in the *Notebooks*, if we read Marthe instead of Lucienne, we find:

> Chapter B1 Recollections. Liaison with Lucienne.
> Chapter B2 Lucienne describes her infidelities.
> Chapter B4 Sexual jealousy. Salzburg. Prague.

It will be noted that the trip and the liaison, by means of sexual jealousy, are linked as effect to cause.

Somewhat later Camus sketches, among his six stories, that of "sexual jealousy." An outline dated August 1937 specifies, in the second part; ". . . Liaison with Catherine . . . Caught in the game. Sexual jealousy. Flight." Catherine now takes the role of Lucienne. But in this same month, another sketch situates the episode of sexual jealousy in the first part, right at the beginning. This episode and that of the trip which follows it then form the essentials of the plot, as this note proves: "Reduce and condense. Story of sexual jealousy which leads to departure. Return to life." Later, when Marthe's name has been adopted, the two episodes are again united; this results in a partial outline

1 Liaison with Marthe . . .
2 Marthe describes her infidelities
3 Innsbruck and Salzburg operetta
                        the letter and the room
                        departure with fever

The heading "Liaison with Marthe" is followed by a bracket in which can be made out, among several names, that of Othello. Did Camus want to make some reference to Shakespeare's study of jealousy? A curious text, which begins with "O! beware, my lord, of jealousy / It is the green-ey'd monster" suggests as much. But Camus will decide that Iago, Desdemona, and the Moor of Venice have nothing to do with Algiers, where Mersault walks with Marthe on his arm. Moreover, he will reduce the importance of this affair and cut it by the trip to central Europe. The only trace of the old connection, at the end of the first part, is found in the letter breaking off the affair.

Of this third chapter two manuscripts exist, one for the first pages, down to "all the shame and humiliation that had been awakened in Mersault's angry heart," and the penultimate paragraph, down to ". . . and after that he went back to visit Zagreus by himself," the rest originally forming the beginning of the chapter devoted to their conversation, the other for the rest of the chapter, from "That was the day Mersault began to be attached to Marthe" to "He wanted to meet him, and his relations with Zagreus began that evening. He saw him frequently, visiting almost every Sunday morning."

page 22, line 7
Ms.: some delicate intoxication, *designating him as its owner in the world's eyes.*

page 23, line 10
Ms.: compared to the *crystalline brilliance of a woman's face, in which all the beauty and futility of the world appears, ultimate luxury of a man's life, given up to (pleasure?) and preoccupation.*

page 24, line 10
Ms.: in his temples *and his eyes go blank.*

page 24, line 13
Ms.: soiled, *transformed into a sordid scene in which rags dangled above garbage.*

page 28, line 10
T.: already asked you not to.
    "Yes, darling."

page 31, line 20
According to Chapter 4, Zagreus is at least fifty; hence it is difficult to imagine that Marthe, though younger than Zagreus, should be young enough for Mersault.

page 32, line 19
Ms.: Rose, Claire, *Catherine.* We may note that Camus's mother was named *Catherine* Sintès.

page 32, line 20
Ms.: Oran

page 34, line 26
Ms. before he spoke. *Then he would speak fast and volubly, generally laughing, but drawing swift conclusions which were always concrete and gave a curious weight of experience to his most trivial jokes. He was alive, that*

was what was striking. This trunk of a man was alive, and in his eyes appeared occasional dim gleams of a kind of concentrated passion which was never melancholy.

Chapter 4

page 36, line 11
Ms.: at the office. *Still I know the secret and ardent life I would have if I had turned into a success, as the saying goes.*

It should be noted that in one of the last outlines, Chapter 2 of Part II is called *"secret and ardent* happiness at Tipasa."

page 36, line 14
Ms.: filled with warmth. *"Listen, Mersault. God knows I'm fond of you. And you've already told me . . ."*

"Yes," Mersault said. "Win or lose. I've lost, and that just suits my laziness."

page 36, line 21
Ms.: Zagreus smiled *and said abruptly: "You're the cripple, my friend," and went on while Mersault blushed: "You live like an idiot, and you think you're smart."*

page 39, line 1
Ms.: sun bakes it. *The sun is the real mirror of the world.*

page 39, line 15
Ms.: body's limits (a kind of promise of happiness)

page 39, line 16
Ms.: But *I couldn't care less about self-knowledge.*

page 40, line 5
Ms.: (opening like a bottomless pit into which Mersault felt himself being dragged)

The preceding sentences in this paragraph do not appear in the manuscript.

page 40, line 9
This sentence is added to the typescript.

page 40, line 14
Ms.: *And yet I feel entirely consonant with this human (and desperate and protean) image of the world which is my own life.*

page 40, line 22
This last phrase is added to the typescript.

page 40, line 24
Ms.: smiled, *as though pleased at having guessed right.*

page 40, line 28
Ms.: can stand, *have killed my will to happiness.*

page 44, line 2
Purity of heart is one of the major problems in Camus. He attempts to distinguish it from virtue (see the end of Chapter 4, Part II: "in the innocence of his heart," taken up like a refrain). Kierkegaard annoyed Camus by linking it with virtue or goodness: "Purity of heart for K. is unity. But it is unity *and* the good." (*Notebooks*, II, p. 55) Camus's entire moral development is located within this problematic conjunction.

page 44, line 14
In the manuscript, Zagreus refers to the loss of his legs in the war (it is to be recalled that Camus's father was mortally wounded in the battle of the Marne). The reference to the First World War was crossed out in the second typescript and replaced by "the accident."

page 45
According to the *Notebooks*, I, p. 21, it is apparently the novel's hero who plays with the revolver.

Chapter 5

A number of texts—typescripts, manuscripts, documents from previously printed sources—draw on, transpose, and scarcely alter Camus's family circle and its situation in the description of the barrelmaker Cardona, a "voice from the workingmen's neighborhood" transcribed with particular concern for autobiographical veracity.

Part Two

Conscious
Death

Chapter 1

The trip to Central Europe, complicated by a love affair, violently affected Camus's sensibility. Prague, for him, represented exile, the wrong side (*"l'envers"*) of the kingdom. It will therefore come as no surprise that this first chapter—an elaborated extract of a travel journal—was prepared from several texts. One figures in *L'Envers et l'Endroit* ("The Wrong Side and the Right Side") under the title "La Mort dans l'âme" ("Death in the Soul"). According to a manuscript version of this particular text, the description of the dead man in the street has been transposed from Algiers, where it actually was observed, to the city of exile; this manuscript is designated here by Ms. 1.

page 57, line 1
Ms.: the man (Mersault)

page 67, line 5
Ms.: against their own demons (against the cruel grimaces of life)

page 69, line 16
Ms. 1: left cheek. *He seemed dead drunk.*

page 69, line 22
Ms. 1: a kind of wild *Sioux* dance

page 69, line 25
Ms. 1: from the nearby restaurant. *It was eleven o'clock, on Christmas night . . . Despite* the rather oppressive interplay of light and shadow, *there was something about the scene that was not fierce and barbaric but instead a kind of primitive innocence.*

page 70, line 1

Ms. 1: everything would collapse *until it could be under-stood without effort.*

And in fact everything would soon be explained. The police were coming. The body was not that of a drunk, but of a dead man, his friend dancing around him.

Only half an hour before, they had knocked at the door of a little restaurant in the neighborhood. They had already had too much to drink and wanted something to eat. But it was Christmas night, and no restaurant had room for them. Though shown the door, they had insisted, and been thrown out. Then they had kicked the proprietress, who happened to be pregnant. And the proprietor, a delicate, blond young man, had picked up a gun and fired. The bullet had lodged in the man's right temple. The head was turned so that it rested on the wound. *Drunk and terror-stricken, the friend had begun dancing.*

The episode was simple enough, and would end tomorrow with an article in the newspaper, but for the moment, in this remote corner, between the faint light on the moist pavement, the long wet hiss of passing cars a few steps away, the distant screech of occasional streetcars, *the scene acquired the disturbing quality of another world:* the insipid *and disturbing image of this neighborhood. When twilight fills the streets with shadows, a single anonymous ghost indicated by a faint sound of footsteps and a confused murmur of voices sometimes appears, haloed by the red light from a pharmacy lamp . . .*

The manuscript ends here.

page 71, line 2

Cf. the newspaper that Meursault, in *The Stranger*, finds in his cell, between the mattress and the bedsprings, in which he reads the story which is the source of *Cross-Purposes* (*Le Malentendu*).

page 71, line 12
Ms.: *silence into which he drained as though into sleep.*

Chapter 2

page 72, line 29
Ms.: take it. (At the Austrian border, the customs officers wakened him from a kind of shapeless dream. Because of it and doubtless too because of his haggard features Mersault had to undergo a lengthy questioning. His papers were minutely examined . . .)

page 75, line 11
Ms.: an image of the ungrateful *and desolate* world
T.: a *symbol* of the ungrateful . . .

page 77, line 18
T.: What are you up to? *Whence do you come? What are you? Whither do you go?*

page 78, line 23
T.: The House *above the World*

page 78, line 27
T.: re-enlisting; *subscribing to L'Illustration.*

page 79
The sojourn in Genoa actually dates from the autumn of 1937, a year later. In fictional elaboration, it is located just after Prague.

page 81, line 22
This sentence does not figure in the manuscript. Camus had noted it on a separate sheet.

page 81, line 29
Ms.: vanity, *the strongest link of all*

page 82, line 28
Ms.: to be run. *He had won his right to happiness.*

Chapter 3

No manuscript of this chapter has been found except for a passage concerning Lucienne contained in a fragment of *Notebooks, I* (pp. 81–2) relating to Marthe. All the variants are taken from the typescript.

page 89, line 4
But Rose intervened, *always ready to defend Claire.*

page 97, line 26
immerses her *in a calm that floods her soul.*

page 103, line 3
keep their *truths.*

page 103, line 5
Instead of the passage beginning "Rose comes over to the parapet . . .": "He loves what is the world in her, if not what is the woman. She yields her whole weight to him, nestling her warmth in the hollow of Patrice's shoulder. He murmurs: 'It will be difficult, but that's no reason.'

" 'No,' Catherine says, her eyes filled with the stars."

Chapter 4

There exists one manuscript version of this entire chapter, as well as a manuscript page of a passage concerning Lucienne and two manuscript sheets of the first dialogue between Patrice and Catherine. The variants taken from the separate manuscript sheets are designated as Ms. 2.

The portion of this chapter up to Patrice's departure from the House above the World has been inserted. Originally the chapter began with the marriage to Lucienne and the dialogue with Catherine.

page 107, line 15
Ms. 2: Catherine had asked.

"*I'm not happy. I have been happy, little girl, but now I'm like a sponge squeezed dry, all shriveled up.*"

page 107, line 21
Ms. 2: for themselves. *But what's the good of cheating? What they want is to love, or to be loved. I'm old enough to have that to look forward to.*"

page 107, line 21
Ms. 2: *Men who are tired of loving don't deserve to be loved. If I was tired of this face filled with light that the world can show me, which smiles today in the sky and on the water, I wouldn't deserve the world.*"

page 107, line 26
Ms. 2: "*What I'd like,*" she said, "*is that you would always do whatever you do without thinking of me.*"

Patrice turned around, his hand on the window latch, and sincerely: "*I'm not thinking about you, little girl. I'd rather not lie. I haven't thought about love for one minute. Understand me—if I'm telling you this, it's because I respect you. Being afraid to make you suffer would be a way of not respecting you.*"

"*Yes,*" Catherine said. "*Thank you.*"

page 108, line 4
Ms. 2: white birds. *Now he could see the tears filling her eyes as she stared at him, and he felt rising within him an immense tide of tenderness without love. He took her hands . . .*

page 108, line 13
Ms. 2: shoulder. "*I have love.*"

page 108, line 17
Ms. 2: strangely hard. *Incapable of loving, of shedding a single tear, what right did he have to speak of love in the name of nothing but love of life.*

page 108, line 24
Ms. 2: and flowers. *But that was what he was compelled to by the blind, black god he would henceforth serve.*

page 113, line 26
Ms.: ask of you. *For the rest, the same youth which has brought us together will separate us someday. There's more for me to do."*

page 118, line 23
T. adapt himself to everything. (endure life, test it, which continued in his flesh and in his darkness. Of course. But he had to want to endure it and to apply his will to the point of no longer having any. That was everything.)

page 123, line 9
Ms.: capacity for *silence*

page 123, line 19
Ms.: He *knew*

page 127, line 1
Ms.: (Claire, Rose, and Catherine)

page 132, line 16
Ms.: better now. *Act in order to be happy: If I have to settle down do it here in a place I like.*

page 132, line 21
Ms.: not forcing ourselves *for other people.*

page 132, line 30
Ms.: hoped it would.
   "Oh, it's all right that way. A man's destiny is never anything but a secret pain."

page 133, line 18
Ms.: with nature. *Unless," he went on, staring at Mersault,*

"unless you've come here the way you withdraw from the world before achieving some great project that will be the meaning of your life."

"For me," Mersault said, "what seems great is the withdrawing. All the rest is politics."

page 134, line 3
Ms.: or on a tremendous *secret."*

page 135, line 7
Apparently in the early sketches for the novel, Camus anticipated his hero would discuss his hopes of his literary vocation. There exists a sketch for the third part (*Notebooks*, I, p. 13) in which he confides in Catherine:

Chapter 1: "Catherine," says Patrice, "I know that now I am going to write. The story of the condemned man. I have come back to my real function, which is to write."

page 135, line 10
Ms.: *"Goodbye, darling," Lucienne said.*

page 135, line 11
Ms.: Three *four*

Chapter 5
___

The manuscript of this chapter consists of pages of various sizes. Apparently it was composed in several stages, from various sources, for example the first paragraph which prefigures the text of "Les Amandiers" ("The Almond Trees") in *L'Été* (*Summer*).

page 139, line 11
Ms.: his own body too, *and followed it inwardly, but with the same truth as* . . .

page 144, line 6
Ms.: a kind of eternity *of flesh*

page 145, line 10
Ms.: he was *hardened to pain*

page 146, line 18
Ms.: you can stay. *Only don't talk."*

page 146, line 20
Ms.: left. *Night was falling.*

page 146, line 27
Ms.: amazing."
"What's going to happen to me?" Lucienne asked.
"Nothing," Mersault said.

page 147, line 20
T.: impotence, *all those who had not been able to find eternity in the flesh*

page 149, line 27
Ms.: this moment *when he realized how little freedom it had*, his body
T.: this moment *when he felt it so close to him*, his body

page 150, line 10
Ms.: cowardice, *far from the touching and tragic comfort whose crucifixes people Europe.*

In Malraux's first novel, Camus could have read: "Of course there is a higher faith, the faith proposed by all the village crucifixes, and those same crosses which stand over our dead. That faith is love, and there is consolation in it. I shall never accept it."

The last sentences of the novel were carefully reworked and recombined. There are many variants—in particular, at the very end, the manuscript phrase: stone among the stones, he returned (to the immobility of real things) to the truth of the motionless worlds.

J. S.

Albert Camus was born in Mondovi, Algeria,
in 1913. He wrote *A Happy Death* between 1936
and 1938, but put the novel aside and the following
year published in Algeria a first book of essays,
L'Envers et L'Endroit. It was in 1942 in occupied
France that *The Myth of Sisyphus* and *The Stranger*
were published and brought him to the attention
of intellectual circles. Among his other major writings
are the essay *The Rebel* and three widely praised
works of fiction, *The Plague*, *The Fall*, and *The Exile
and the Kingdom*. He also published a volume of
plays, *Caligula and Three Other Plays*, as well as
various dramatic adaptations. In 1957 Camus was
awarded the Nobel Prize for Literature. On January 4,
1960, he was killed in an automobile accident.

A Note on the Type

This book was set on the Linotype in Janson, a recutting made direct from type cast from matrices long thought to have been made by the Dutchman Anton Janson, who was a practicing type founder in Leipzig during the years 1668–87. However, it has been conclusively demonstrated that these types are actually the work of Nicholas Kis (1650–1702), a Hungarian, who most probably learned his trade from the master Dutch type founder Dirk Voskens. The type is an excellent example of the influential and sturdy Dutch types that prevailed in England up to the time William Caslon developed his own incomparable designs from them.

The book was composed, printed, and bound by Kingsport Press, Inc., Kingsport, Tennessee. Typography and binding design by Betty Anderson.